More by the Author

Horror

Dissonance Junction

From the Shadows

The Dark Collective

Granny Bael

Immortal (The Haunting of Orchard House)

Anthologies

Monstrosity (Unnerving Anthology, Vol. 1)

Descent (Unnerving Anthology, Vol. 2)

Eclipse (Unnerving Anthology, Vol. 3)

Wicked (Unnerving Anthology, Vol. 4)

The Mighty Pen

Tales of the Slug

UNDEAD RECKONING

LAUREN PATZER

BLUE FORGE PRESS
Port Orchard, Washington

Blue Forge Press is the print division of the volunteer-run, federal 501(c)3 nonprofit company, Blue Legacy, founded in 1989 and dedicated to bringing light to the shadows and voice to the silence. We strive to empower storytellers across all walks of life with our four divisions: Blue Forge Press, Blue Forge Films, Blue Forge Gaming, and Blue Forge Records. Find out more at www.MyBlueLegacy.org

Blue Forge Press
7419 Ebbert Drive Southeast
Port Orchard, Washington 98367
blueforgepress@gmail.com
360-550-2071 ph.txt

*I fully recognize the impact
a lack of mental health services
has had on our society,
from crime and homelessness
to suicide and hopelessness.
I dedicate this novel
to those who seek solutions
and treatment for themselves,
their loved ones, or society in general.*

UNDEAD RECKONING

LAUREN PATZER

CHAPTER 1

*M*artin Simon checked his bright red tie in the driver's side mirror just for a split second before he turned to the Alvarez family standing behind him with a winning smile. "Now, this is one of the newest hybrid designs getting the best rating for emissions control. It blows away the state requirements and it's the smoothest ride you will ever take. A smooth ride is important, right?" Martin asked as he winked at the pregnant mother. Her husband nodded and put his arm protectively around her.

Martin wasn't sure if the move was simply to protect her from harm or make sure she didn't fall for the handsome, athletically-built salesman. He made a mental note to pare down the flirtation quotient and emphasize safety, then Martin opened the driver's side door and gestured for the couple to look inside the brand new sport utility vehicle.

Behind Martin, a plain-looking sedan pulled into the dealership's visitor parking. Two men in plain suits got out and took a brief look around before heading inside. They were both lanky, but one was taller than the other. The shorter one walked with a bit of stiffness to his gait. Martin gave them a quick glance and frowned before returning his attention to the couple looking at the car.

"Mister Alvarez, let me demonstrate just how easy it is to put in a baby seat," he said as he opened the door behind the driver's seat. The couple moved to get a better look. Martin again gave a quick glance at the two men in the dealership as they walked forward, noting their gait and direction they traveled. The shorter one had brown hair while the taller one, presumably older and the senior of the two, had gray hair turning white on the sides. The taller one carried a large notebook in his right hand.

Inside the dealership, Detectives Johnson and Smith walked up to the receptionist's desk. Kelly Marcos looked up from her computer screen and smiled at them. Her bright red lipstick complimented the white blouse she wore. The white blouse was tight on her chest, emphasizing her figure. As she lifted her hands off the keyboard, her bright red nails sparkled a bit. Glitter in the polish gave them that tell-tale twinkle. Detective Johnson, the taller of the two, raised an eyebrow.

"How can I help you?" Kelly said with a genuine, warm smile.

"Can you direct me to the manager here?" Detective Johnson asked.

Kelly gave a brief glance behind her toward the middle-aged Hispanic man sitting at a desk, sleeves rolled up, moving his mouse and frowning at the computer screen. She turned back to Detective Johnson and stood up. "Sure thing," Kelly responded. "Mister Denton is the owner and manager. His office is right this way if you'll follow me." Kelly walked carefully in the high heels, her hips swaying gently back and forth, captured in a tight black skirt.

Detective Smithers gave a small cough as he observed

the young woman's figure. Detective Johnson gave him a disapproving glance and Detective Smithers raised his eye line to the back of her head. The men followed the receptionist to Mister Denton's office.

Carlos Denton got up and ran his fingers briefly along the black suspenders holding up dark pleated slacks. As he stepped out from behind the desk, his black patent leather shoes gleamed in the showroom lights. His hair cut was short and professional with just a bit of gleam.

"Mister Denton, these gentlemen were asking to see you," Kelly said as she stopped at the office door.

"Of course," Carlos responded with a smile. "How can I help you, gentlemen?" Carlos greeted them both with a handshake. They handed him their business cards.

Kelly left and Detective Smithers turned to watch her walk away. Detective Johnson cleared his throat and Detective Smithers quickly turned back to face Carlos.

"My apologies, detectives. Having an attractive greeter is but one tool in my arsenal of salesmanship." Carlos shrugged. "She is taken, of course."

"So is he." Detective Johnson smirked. "And I'm married to my job, or so my ex told me."

Carlos gave a wan smile. "So many of us are," Carlos said. "Please, take a seat." He waved at the office chairs. The two detectives took their seats, Smithers appearing stiff as he slowly lowered himself into the chair. Carlos sat back down behind his desk.

"Mister Denton—" Detective Johnson began.

"Please, call me Carlos, Detective."

"Very well, Carlos. We are investigating two tragic deaths in the area and are following any connections we can to these men," Detective Johnson replied as he opened his notebook and pulled a pen from his suit pocket. "One of them, a Howard Ellis, purchased a vehicle from your dealership recently. We'd like to talk to anyone who last saw him here."

"Not a problem. Let me check our records and see who helped Mr. Ellis with his purchase," Carlos replied as he waved at Kelly, who watched them from the reception desk. "Kelly!"

Kelly walked back to the office. "Yes, Carlos?" she asked. Detective Smithers stared straight ahead, not looking toward the attractive woman. He gave a nervous swallow. Kelly noticed and smiled briefly before resuming her businesslike demeanor.

"Can you find the purchase record for a Howard Ellis?" Carlos asked as he turned back to Detective Johnson. "Do you know which vehicle he purchased and when?"

Detective Johnson pulled a single sheet out from a pocket in the notebook and handed it to Carlos.

Carlos perused the paper for a moment and nodded. "Okay. Martin usually handles all SUV sales, so he was likely the sales associate. Kelly, looks like the purchase was October two years ago. Can you look that up for us?"

"Certainly," Kelly replied. She walked back to the receptionist's desk and began typing into her computer.

"I was here, of course. Although, I honestly can't recall everyone who purchased a vehicle here. Kelly was not here back then. Margo Stanwood was here but I believe she's moved overseas with her husband, who's in the military. And the finance manager at the time would have been Denny Clydesdale, who is still in that position. Anyone of several finance assistants under him could have helped. As for Martin…" Carlos said as he turned to look out at the main lot. He pointed at Martin chatting with the Alvarez family next to the SUV. Martin knelt down and pointed to the underside of the car.

"That's Martin there. One of our best sales associates. Started off washing cars here five years ago. His attention to detail is stunning. Worked his way up to sales that same year and was just promoted to sales manager six months ago. He has an uncanny way of recognizing truly talented salespeople. Twenty percent rise in sales since he joined management."

Martin looked up at the Alvarez family as he pointed to the underside of the SUV. "They really beefed up the suspension on this model three years ago. Very solid ride. Five star safety rating for side impact as well, so it is sturdy and safe."

Mister Alvarez put his arm around his pregnant wife's shoulder as she smiled and snuggled into his chest, placing her hands protectively around her tummy.

Kelly walked up to the men as they watched Martin. She handed several papers to Carlos, who took them, examined them closely and nodded. "Yes, definitely Martin. He can sell a vehicle to just about anybody. Would you like to speak to him?"

"That would be helpful," Detective Johnson replied.

"Maybe he can convince you to give up your junker," Detective Smithers followed up with a smirk. Detective Johnson glared at him. "Or maybe not."

Martin walked into the dealership showroom with the Alvarez family close behind.

Carlos waved at Martin. "Martin, could you spare a

moment for these gentlemen?" Carlos called as he stood up. The detectives rose from their seats and turned around.

Martin looked at Carlos and the two men. He smiled and waved. He turned to Kelly as he walked to the reception desk. "Kelly, could you help the Alvarezes with their paperwork while I talk to Carlos and the detectives?" He turned back to the Alvarezes and smiled. "I saw these guys on television. They're fairly new detectives. I've helped law enforcement before on some stolen vehicles. But, I wanted to let you know, the model you've picked is very low on the list for stolen vehicles—the smaller compacts are much more likely to get stolen. You've made a good choice."

Kelly stepped forward with a smile and waved toward Martin's sales office, just a few steps away. "If you would please follow me. Can I get you something to drink? Water, coffee, soft drink?"

"You'll be fine with Kelly. She and I are a close-knit team," Martin said with a confident smile. He'd been working with Kelly for a few weeks after she'd come on. She was his unofficial assistant and he made sure she got a cut of the sales she helped him with. When they could find a new receptionist, she'd be joining his team; he knew she'd be excellent selling the sportier vehicles to the young men who stopped by the dealership.

As they walked away, Martin clenched his jaw for a moment before fixing a smile on his face. He reflexively touched his hair to ensure it was as immaculate as it was when he'd walked the Alvarez family out to the lot. He turned toward his boss and strode confidently to the group of men who had now stepped out of the office, standing just outside it. As he approached them, he held out his hand. "Martin

Simon," he said as he shook their hands. "How can I help two of L.A.'s finest?"

"How did you know we're police?" Detective Smithers asked.

"Let's see," Martin said as he faced Detective Smithers. "I saw you on a newscast about three weeks ago. I think it was a missing child case—girl about fourteen years of age, if I'm not mistaken. You found her, I believe."

"Yes, thankfully unharmed," Detective Smithers said as he nodded. "Amazing."

Martin faced Detective Johnson. "And you were on the news sixteen months ago, standing behind the chief of police at a news conference about an unsolved murder you were looking for tips on—"

"The Handyman serial killer," Detective Johnson finished.

"That's right, now I remember." Martin nodded. "And I found it curious at the time that the FBI hadn't taken over the investigation."

"We're in consultation with many other branches of law enforcement on multiple cases, but I'm afraid we can't share more specifics than that," Detective Johnson said.

"Of course not," Martin replied and looked down. "I didn't mean to imply you should."

"You have a pretty impressive memory, Mr. Simon," Detective Smithers observed.

"Please, call me Martin. I have a semi-photographic memory. It really helps in sales to connect with the customers. But, I can only remember what I hear or see. I didn't get your names, so I know you're detectives, but..."

"I'm Detective Johnson and this is Detective Smithers.

We're here to ask a few questions about a murder victim who may have been a customer of yours."

"Well, that's a shame. Never know when your time is up, do you?"

Detective Smithers showed Howard Ellis' picture to Martin, who looked at the picture for a moment and then looked up in thought. "Ah, Howard Ellis. Good customer. Credit rating was 705, I believe. Purchased a top of the line SUV, including an extended warranty with a loan from First Element Credit Union, connected to his work as a chemical engineer. He was shopping with his wife... no, it was a woman and her child. I don't know if they were married. She didn't complete any paperwork."

"Common-law wife and their daughter," Detective Smithers offered.

In Martin's mind, he was parked in a car across the street from the Ellis household. He looked in through the living room window and observed as Howard Ellis backhanded his wife with his right hand, knocking her to the ground. Their eight-year-old daughter cowered in a corner nearby, shaking and screaming.

Martin looked back down at the picture. "Really nice family. They seemed so happy," he said.

"Not so happy," Detective Smithers said. "History of spousal abuse."

Martin cocked his head. "Really?" He shook his head. "That's a shame. Well, I can only remember what I see or hear. It doesn't mean I'm a good judge of character, obviously."

Martin's mind returned to his interaction with the family sitting across from him in his office. The wife wore sunglasses even though it was dark outside. There was the merest hint of a bruise under her right eye, covered by thick makeup. She pulled her sleeves down when one inched up, revealing a bruise on her arm. Martin noted all the details wordlessly, smiling as Howard signed the paperwork, right-handed.

Martin smiled at the detectives. "What can I do to help?" he asked.

"Mister Ellis' body was found near another body. Have you seen this man?" Detective Johnson asked as Detective Smithers handed another picture of a gentleman older than Howard Ellis to Martin.

The older gentleman brought a memory to Martin's mind. The victim stood up from his table in a restaurant setting and, using his right hand, shoved a waiter, knocking the employee down. The lady at the table with the older man appeared visibly upset. Martin watched from a nearby table, calmly eating his food even as he took in every detail. The older gentleman left the restaurant alone, leaving a flustered date crying at the table. Martin handed his own server a hundred-dollar bill.

"That should cover everything," he said as he stood up and left the restaurant.

"Thank you very much, sir," the server replied to Martin's back as he hurried out of the restaurant.

Martin handed the photograph back to Detective Smithers. "I can't say as I recognize him," Martin replied. "Was he a customer here as well? We could check the records."

"We have no reason to believe he was," Detective Johnson replied, shaking his head. "We just thought maybe the two were connected somehow. Just tracking down leads."

"I understand," Martin replied and looked at his boss. "Carlos, could we look and see if he was a customer, just to check?"

"We only have his name," Detective Johnson said, holding up his hands. "There's no car trail leading back here."

"Well..." Martin stroked his chin thoughtfully. "Maybe he stopped in to look for a car but never purchased one. We may have run a credit report on him and we keep records of all those transactions."

"Here's his information," Detective Johnson said as he handed another sheet of paper to Carlos.

"I'll run this and get right back to you," Carlos replied as he walked to his office and typed information into his own computer.

"Detective Smithers," Martin said, turning to the younger officer. "I noticed you stand favoring your right side. Are you having a little back trouble?"

Detective Smithers reflexively put his hand on his back, but then quickly put it back down. "You're very observant," he said.

"We have several models with excellent lumbar support. Heated seats too," Martin said with a genuine smile.

"Are you always looking to make a sale?" Detective Johnson asked, eyebrows raised.

"Law enforcement personnel are just as entitled as the average citizen to drive a quality vehicle. Here, take my card." Martin handed his business cards to them. "If you're looking for a new or used vehicle, just give me a call. Our dealership actually has a public service employee discount."

"I'll be sure to do that," Detective Smithers said.

Carlos returned with a frown and a shrug. "I'm afraid he was never even a potential customer here."

"That's all right. Thank you for checking, just the same. Could you direct us to Mister Clydesdale?"

"I'm afraid he's not in today, but will return tomorrow. He's in Tahoe, I believe, with his family," Carlos replied.

"Very good," Detective Johnson replied. "We'll drop back in tomorrow just to cover all the bases. Thank you both for your cooperation."

The detectives shook hands with Martin and Carlos and left the building. Martin walked over to his office and poked his head in, checking on the Alvarez family still working with Kelly to complete the paperwork.

"Everything all right here?" Martin asked.

Kelly looked up with a smile. "We're almost done," she said and pointed at the bottom of the page Mister Alvarez was looking at. "Just sign there."

"Great, I will be right back in a few minutes and we'll get those keys ready for you, okay?" Martin asked.

"That sounds great," Mister Alvarez replied as Kelly turned another page and pointed again at the signature block on the paperwork.

"Perfect," Martin responded with a smile as he ducked back out of the office and walked calmly to the rear of the showroom to the family bathroom. He walked in and locked the door behind him. He frantically washed his hands and splashed cold water on his face.

Martin looked up at the mirror as the memory of him stabbing the older gentleman in the back with two knives flooded his mind. As the victim screamed and fell to the ground, Martin quickly double checked his surgical gloves to ensure they were still intact. He bent over the older gentleman and cut the right-hand sleeve of the jacket and shirt all the way open. He held up the right arm and presses the blade against the elbow joint.

Less than an hour later, he was dumping the body in the same place Howard Ellis was laid to rest. He remembered standing over the spot for more than ten minutes, just staring down in the ravine. It was dark and he couldn't see anything, but his mind had the two men's faces staring back at him from out of the dark. They growled at him and he smiled. He flipped the visions off and went back to his car.

Martin looked down as he dried off his face. He took a deep breath to steady his nerves. They'd never been this close. He'd never gotten so much as a parking ticket in his adult years. He did the mental calculations of those he'd met at the dealership who had later found themselves on the business end of his blade. There were three over five years. If the others were never found, this incident would just be a fluke. No reason for the detectives to return to take a second look at him.

He looked in the mirror and blinked a few times just to anchor himself in the present. He quickly examined his clothing and removed any pieces of lint or paper towel from his suit. He checked his hair and looked his face over for any signs of moisture or left over towel. He wiped down the sink and counter, paying extra attention to some dried soap on the counter. He examined the rest of the bathroom and determined it was clean enough. With a quick look in the mirror again, he smiled and walked out of the bathroom.

CHAPTER 2

*M*artin stood in his immaculate kitchen dressed in a white shirt, beige fleur-de-lis tie and gray slacks polishing a large knife over the sink. He held the blade up to the light and meticulously polished any blemish he saw. Arrayed on the counter were another five knives of the same brand, all large enough to hack flesh from bone or easily liberate a forearm from the rest of the body.

The kitchen counter was a study in efficiency and obsessive-compulsive disorder. Various kitchen appliances and utensil holders were evenly spaced along the spotless backsplash of white ceramic tiles. The bright white granite counter was so polished it gave a perfect reflection of the overhead circular fluorescent light fixtures.

To Martin's left, through an opening on the counter that led to the living room, which was similarly arranged as if purchased from a *Feng Shui* catalog, the television blared the local newscast.

Local newscaster Lisa Cox smiled at the camera as a helicopter shot appeared behind her, showing several police vehicles and personnel at the edge of a deep canyon wall. Some people repelled down the side of the canyon wall. A few white tarps covered two human shaped piles next to the vehicles.

"In a chilling turn of events, police located two more victims of the Handyman killer in a rural canyon in Riverside yesterday," Lisa reported.

"You missed one then," Martin murmured as he continued to polish the knife.

"Police are hoping these new victims will turn up some forensic evidence to help them in their hunt for the prolific serial killer," Lisa continued.

"Not likely," Martin replied as he held the knife up to the light and examined the blade one more time.

"Even without that, police are concentrating on a recent development that could put them closer to the suspect."

Martin turned his head to look at the television.

"In an exclusive for Eyewitness Daily News, according to unnamed sources, a potential witness has come forward, claiming he saw the killer as he was committing one of his crimes," Lisa said as the camera angle switched to show her from a different side. The graphic behind her changed to a logo the news channel had used before to represent the Handyman Killer—a bloody knife and a disembodied hand freshly cut by the blade, minus the blood.

Martin pulled a leather case from a satchel on the ground next to the counter. He rolled out the leather case and placed the knives in custom designed slots as he watched the television.

"Do continue, Lisa," Martin said. "You have my nearly uninterrupted attention."

"A video recently appeared on the video-sharing

website 'Now You See It,'" Lisa continued. A video appeared full screen of an older, white-haired Hispanic man wearing a black shirt open at the collar, staring at the camera. The background was an indistinct white sheetrock wall common in any house or apartment.

"I saw him murder my granddaughter from my apartment window. It happened right down there in the parking lot," the old man began and seemed to tear up. "I don't have a phone and it's very hard for me to get around. I never saw any police. My granddaughter was reported missing, but the police didn't work very hard to solve the case. I couldn't bring myself to talk to the police due to my grief. But I think I will be able to come forward soon."

The video cut off and switched back to Lisa with the Handyman Killer logo up on the screen behind her as before. "We contacted the LAPD about this fresh development, but were told they could not comment on an ongoing investigation. The video was pulled shortly after we learned of it here at Eyewitness Daily News. I guess it was a case of now you see it, now you don't. There is no confirmation on whether or not this is a hoax and the man in the video remains unidentified at this time."

The news switched to a male broadcaster and a sports newscast logo behind him. Martin pulled a remote from the drawer in front of him and shut off the television. He carefully placed the remote back in its spot in the drawer and checked everything else to ensure it was all aligned correctly and then he slowly closed the drawer.

"Female likely in her twenties, of Hispanic descent," Martin murmured as he washed the counter off with a sponge. "Apartment... parking lot..."

Martin frowned. The memory came up of a young woman who had beaten up an old lady and stolen her purse on a street. Martin had been driving by. He'd followed the woman to an apartment complex and staked out her place. But, the murder had happened inside the woman's apartment. He'd loaded her up in the car outside. It had been around 4am in the morning. No screams. He'd been careful, but obviously not careful enough.

"Maria... something. Little more than a street thug. A violent street thug," Martin whispered with closed eyes. Her face came to him, but it was unremarkable. Just a woman's face, Hispanic like many he'd seen before. Maybe too much like his mother's face. He shook his head and blinked his eyes rapidly.

So, the old man had seen a stranger load something into a car the day his granddaughter disappeared. Not a strong legal case and doubly unlikely there was any forensic trail or way to track the vehicle. But a loose end was a loose end.

"Echo Vista," Martin said, as he quickly placed the sponge next to the kitchen faucet. He grabbed his jacket, put the leather case with the knives in the satchel and picked it up. He ran out the front door.

Before the door could close, he ran back in, walked to the kitchen sink and carefully aligned the sponge so it was centered perfectly on the edge of the sink between the faucet and the counter edge. He looked at it for a moment and then took a deep breath. He turned and calmly walked back out the door.

Martin pulled into the visitor parking at the Echo Vista apartment complex. He stepped out of his maroon sedan and straightened his tie. He glanced at his car and noticed a speck of dust on the fender. He went to the trunk, opened it, and took out two rags, a spray bottle and a small container of car wax. He returned to the speck, sprayed a small amount of the water on it and used one rag to clean it off. He then opened the wax, put a small amount of it on another rag and applied it to the spot. He rubbed the wax in until it appeared clear, then used the other end of the rag to polish it to a sparkle.

He stepped back and observed his handiwork. He nodded, put the items back in the trunk, and retrieved his satchel. He closed the trunk and walked to the leasing office door.

As Martin walked into the leasing office, the young blonde woman who sat at the only desk in the room looked up and smiled. She was dressed professionally in a dark grey skirt suit with a white ruffled blouse. She stood and walked easily toward him on a pair of high heels. "Hi, I'm Shelly. Can I help you?" Shelly said as she not so casually looked Martin up and down and raised an eyebrow.

Martin smiled at her and laughed casually as he glanced around the small office, looking for video cameras. There didn't appear to be any. "Well, Shelly, I normally plan my day a little better, but I was driving by and just had an urge to check out these apartments. Is it okay if I look around a bit?" Martin asked.

"Of course," Shelly replied. "Are you looking for a studio, one bedroom or two bedroom?"

"Well, it's just me, so a studio or one bedroom would

be fine, but I'll consider *anything* that's available," Martin replied with a smile.

"Oh, is that right?" Shelly said with a big grin. "Well, I will need a copy of your driver's license and then I can get you a key to our model apartment and a very personal tour."

Martin pulled out his wallet and retrieved the license behind his real one. He'd only used it once before and it hadn't been compromised yet, so he was confident it would keep him anonymous enough even to the smitten leasing agent. He handed it to her with a big smile.

Not so casually, Shelly looked at his fingers for any sign of a ring. She looked at the license and then back up at him. "Well, Jeremy, I hope you find something you like today."

Martin gave her an encouraging smile. She walked into an alcove behind the front room with a little extra sway to her hips. As the copier warmed up, Martin reached for the front of his satchel and stuck his hand inside. The sound of the door opening behind him caused him to pull his hand back out empty-handed and set the satchel down at his side. An elderly gentleman walked in behind him wearing an old sweater and pants pulled up around his rib cage.

"Hey Shelly," the old man hollered. "I'm ready for that tour!"

Shelly rushed out of the alcove with a frown on her face. She looked at the clock and her shoulders fell. She placed the copy of Martin's fake license on her desk and handed him back the actual fake license. "Of course, Mister Winston," Shelly replied. "Just a moment." She turned back to Martin with a grimace. "I'm sorry, Jeremy. I forgot I had an appointment. But I should be done in about twenty minutes," she said as she handed Martin the model apartment key and a site map. Her hand lingered on his as he took the key. "Just remember, you can tell me if anything catches your eye." She winked and Martin smiled again.

"I'll be sure to do that," Martin replied as he lingered on her hand for just a moment. "Is it Shelly or Michelle?"

"Whichever you like better," she whispered. She let go of his hand and turned to Mister Winston. "Let me grab the keys and I'll show you around, okay?" she said a bit loudly.

"All right," Mister Winston replied and turned around to leave.

Shelly went back into the alcove for a moment, and Martin quickly palmed the copy she'd made of his fake license. He pushed another similar-looking page into its place from the other papers on her desk. He turned, walked past Mister Winston and left the building.

Martin walked into the complex through an open pedestrian gate. He looked at the map and headed in the direction of the apartment he had the key for. Shelly and Mister Winston headed out in the opposite direction. Martin disappeared behind one building and stopped. He poked his head out around the building and watched Shelly and Mister Winston walk out of sight behind another building. He looked around for anyone watching and then walked in a new direction to a particular parking area between two buildings.

"One of us dies today, old man," Martin hissed as he walked into the center of the parking lot. He looked up at the windows of the surrounding apartments. Martin scanned the windows, but finally shook his head.

Too many variables, he thought. *Have to go door to door.*

A young Hispanic boy walked up to Martin.

"Hello," Martin said.

"You could try *hola*," the boy said. "Ain't you Mexican?"

"I never learned the language," Martin replied with a shrug.

"Huh. Well, *pendejo*, this is for you. The old man said you'd give me a dollar."

Martin grit his teeth, as he knew Spanish quite well. He took the envelope and smiled. "The old man lied. But I'll give you ten dollars if you tell me where he lives."

The boy squinted at Martin. "How do I know you're not lying?"

Martin pulled out a ten-dollar bill and handed it to the boy. Without hesitation, the boy kicked Martin in the shin and ran away.

"Dammit," Martin groaned as he gave chase, hobbling a bit because of the bruised shin. The boy quickly disappeared and Martin stopped chasing him. He sat down on some stairs and rubbed his shin. He looked at the envelope and sighed. He opened it up and looked at the address. It was in the hills nearly an hour away.

I think that's an abandoned industrial area, Martin thought as he closed his eyes and brought up a mental map of the area. Way up in the hills, abandoned for years because of the danger of landslides in the area. It was very secluded.

He heard a car start up and pull out of the parking lot just across from him. He caught a glimpse of the driver, who bore more than a passing resemblance to the old man in the video. The car was an old white sedan; it was dusty and Martin remembered passing it earlier and suppressing an urge to wash it.

"Game on, old man," Martin whispered as he stuffed the envelope into his pocket. He ran back to the front of the complex, rushing past Shelly and Mister Winston. He tossed the model key toward Shelly as he ran by. Shelly bent down and retrieved the key.

"Jeremy!" Shelly shouted. "Call me!"

Martin left them behind without responding. He raced around the leasing office and jumped into his car. He started it up and backed up quickly. He pulled out into the street and looked both ways, but didn't catch sight of the old man who had driven away.

He pulled the envelope out of his pocket. *Well, at least I know where you're going.*

Martin pulled to the side of the road, stopped the car and got out. He walked around the car and caught a splotch of bird droppings on the roof. He went to his trunk and repeated the cleaning process he'd done earlier, leaving the surface of the car roof pristine and freshly waxed.

As he stood there looking at the car, his mind traveled back to a time when an eight-year-old Martin was being yelled at by his stepfather in the garage. The older white man pointed at a car in the driveway. There were cleaning rags, soap and a hose nearby. The car finish sparkled in the sunlight, like it had just been driven off the showroom floor.

"You call that clean? That car is filthy!" his stepfather *screamed. He raised his right hand and backhanded Martin. The young boy flew across the garage and hit the wall so hard that he couldn't catch his breath when he fell to the ground. His lungs ached as he tried to suck in enough air to keep from blacking out.*

"Clean it again, you worthless spic! No wonder your spic

father ran out on you! Couldn't get a decent price for you in the tomato fields, I guess." The man stepped over him to get to a fridge by the door and grabbed a cold beer. *"Do it again or there's no dinner for your worthless ass tonight."*

Martin shook his head and was back in the modern day. He walked around his car again three times as he meticulously checked it over and finally found it acceptably clean. He walked back to the trunk, opened it up and put the rags back in a plastic garbage bag next to the spare tire. The remainder of his tools inventory included a coffee can, some lighter fluid, a long barbecue lighter and bleach wipes. They were all neatly arranged within plastic boxes taped down to the floor of the trunk, which was lined with a black tarp.

Martin walked back to the passenger side of the car, opened it up and retrieved the satchel. As he placed the satchel in the trunk and shut the trunk, he took a deep breath to flush the unwelcome memory from his mind entirely. He got back into the car and started it up.

CHAPTER 3

The old white sedan rolled over the broken asphalt of the old parking lot outside a two story red brick warehouse structure. Broken windows dotted the side of the structure and an old sign hung halfway attached to the building, touching the ground. The severely rusted sign made it hard to discern what the old building had been in a past life. Despite its state of decay, the abandoned and remote building served Hiram Salvatore's needs just fine.

Hiram stepped out of the car and walked around to the back of the trunk, favoring his left side. A brace on the outside of his faded black pants held his right knee in place — an injury that had slowed him down and eventually stopped his own extracurricular activities. He had a similar hobby to Martin's escapades. He looked around for a moment, then dug a couple pills from his pocket and popped them into his mouth.

Only a short while longer, he thought as he opened the trunk and pulled out a medium-sized duffle bag. He closed the trunk and shuffled into the old building.

As he passed into the building, the sunlight filtered in through broken windows, illuminating the dust in the air.

Hiram paused and closed his eyes. He was a younger man back in his apartment and a ten-year-old Hispanic girl ran around as he played tag with her.

She giggled and jumped around on the furniture, doing everything to escape him. Finally, he tagged her and shouted, "You're it!"

The little girl chased him around the apartment as Hiram jumped over furniture, replicating her flight from him. He ran his right knee into a coffee table and fell to the floor, grabbing the injured knee. The little girl immediately ran to his side.

"*Abuelito!*" she cried as she stopped next to him, her little forehead furrowed with concern. "Are you okay?"

"*Si*, Maria," Hiram reassured her as he rubbed his knee. "But maybe we switch to playing checkers now, okay?"

"Okay!" she responded with an enthusiastic hug.

Back in the dusty building, Hiram coughed and wrinkled his nose. He looked to his right and climbed the stairs to the second floor.

Martin drove up the winding road and passed a familiar landmark–a twisting sign showing curves up ahead. The significance of the landmark wasn't the warning to other drivers, but the marker for another of Martin's kills.

Three months ago, on a night warmed by the Santa Ana winds blowing constantly, Martin stood on the side of the road looking at an array of rocks lining the side of the canyon wall. In his arms, he held the motionless body of a young woman in her mid-twenties. Her hair was pristine outside of the blood that had sprayed onto it during her recent passing. Her right forearm was absent.

Martin glanced back at his maroon sedan with a mixed breed dog sitting in the passenger side seat. One of his eyes was missing and, if he'd jumped out of the car, he would've done so with a limp. The woman he held led a frustrated life and took it out on her canine companion. In a continuation of her bad luck, she'd beaten her best friend in view of Martin sitting inside a coffee shop on Santa Monica Boulevard. She kept the dog on the leash and dragged it back toward her again and again to hit it. As Martin stood up, intent on stopping her attack on the animal, she must've hit the poor dog just right and knocked it unconscious. She picked it up and carried it away like a sack of potatoes. There was no remorse on her face, just disgust at having to carry the unconscious animal.

Now she was in Martin's arms, the offending limb removed. It hadn't taken him long to determine her movements and find a time when she'd be vulnerable to his own attack. He'd been relieved to see the dog still alive when he'd seen her exit her home, taking the dog for a walk. It was three blocks before she passed near Martin's parked vehicle, a route she always repeated during the evening walk. The neighborhood was dark at this time of night. He was here three nights in a row and the neighbors rarely looked outside. As far as he could tell, none of them had dogs that were outside at night either. He reckoned they kept the animals inside to provide for their owners' safety.

He'd simply come up behind the animal abuser and choked her out until she was unconscious. Her body wrapped in a tarp made a dull thud as he dropped it in his trunk. She was still alive, but Martin was conscious of forensic evidence and wanted to reduce the amount he'd have to clean up.

Hooks he welded inside the rim of the trunk held another tarp in place. When he picked up the docile dog and put him in the passenger seat, the dog didn't bark once or even whine.

Once they reached their destination, Martin removed the offending limb and wrapped it in a burlap sack for transport to his secret trophy case. She lost consciousness again due to blood loss. Martin reasoned he treated her as humanely as she treated her dog. After he heaved her body past the rocks and it tumbled down into the canyon, he glanced at the dog again; it simply cocked its head at him.

Was it thankful or just curious?

Martin dropped the wounded canine off outside a shelter, tied up to the door handle about an hour before the place opened. No one connected the dog to the victim because she'd never registered or even chipped the animal, giving it the barest essentials of care.

It happened months ago, but it seemed just like yesterday to Martin. He rocketed past the sign and looked at the dashboard clock. The digital readout displayed it was just after four o'clock.

"Rest in pieces, Rebecca," Martin said as he gripped the wheel tighter.

Twenty minutes later, Martin pulled his car alongside the white sedan he'd seen leaving the apartment building. He looked around and scratched his head.

Not optimal for a police ambush, he thought as he opened the car door. Just the same, he walked around to both sides of the building. The road leading behind was over grown and full of debris. There likely weren't any vehicles lying in wait behind the building.

Martin returned to the car and took off his suit coat.

He folded it up neatly and set it on the passenger side seat. It took him several adjustments before he was satisfied with its orientation on the seat, perfectly centered on all sides.

He went to the trunk and opened his satchel. Before he went any further, he pulled on surgical gloves and examined them to ensure they were fully intact. Satisfied with the glove integrity, he pulled the knife case out and retrieved a custom designed leather vest that held four knives, two in front and two in back that he could easily reach. He put the vest on and sheathed the knives in it. As he adjusted the vest and knives, he thought about the fake name and bank account he set up to get the vest ordered. As far as he knew, no one had tried tracing them, but it was only a matter of time before someone started sniffing around. His mind wandered to the two Detectives who visited the dealership.

They're far off base, but uncomfortably close.

Perhaps it had been foolish to succumb to the compulsion to remove Howard Ellis from the living.

Fewer people deserved it more than that scumbag.

Martin closed the trunk and took a deep breath to focus. He took another look around and remained convinced there was no surveillance. He stepped up to the front door and looked at a new handwritten sign taped to the broken window.

'Help Wanted: Handyman, Inquire Within'

"Funny," Martin mumbled as he quietly opened the door and stepped inside.

The hiring manager is in for a rude awakening.

Detective Johnson flipped through the report and scratched his head. Across from him, Special Agent Hank Jansen from the FBI sat patiently, looking at his phone. Agent Jansen's freshly pressed suit, black tie and white shirt gave the typical impression of an FBI agent.

"This really doesn't put us much closer to the Handyman," Detective Johnson said. "Male between twenty and fifty who may have been the victim of child abuse growing up? That's a couple million just in LA County."

"He's meticulous, though. Very thorough. No DNA at any crime scene. Micro inspection of the wounds suggests a similar weapon is used in each murder, but the striations in the wound patterns are inconsistent. He may sharpen the blade between each use, changing the profile of the blade edge," Agent Jansen said, and then looked up from his phone. "And he's local, given his knowledge of the area to plan dumping sites well out of eyesight."

"Age, sex, he's a careful killer and local," Detective Johnson said. "Like I said, that doesn't narrow things down much."

"The removal of the right forearm is a signature, but it's the only one we can link between the victims, of which we've only found six we can even confirm are definitely his. You have thousands of missing persons in this county alone. Find more confirmed victims, identify them and maybe we can develop a more targeted profile. Keep in mind you can still use these criteria to evaluate anyone connected to the case. You may have met the killer already and didn't realize it."

"What if he hasn't killed any other people?" Detective Johnson asked as he tapped his pen nervously on the report.

"Besides the twenty we suspect? Oh, he's killed more," Agent Jansen said as he stood up. "The ones you've found are the tip of the iceberg."

"Have you been able to track down the maker of the video yet?"

"Court orders take time and the video hosting company has been uncooperative until we do so," Agent Jansen sighed. "It also may be a hoax. The video didn't go up until weeks after your news conference."

"That garnered worse than useless tips."

Detective Smithers opened the door.

"Detective?" Agent Jansen asked.

"We just got an anonymous tip and you will not believe who they told us to look at," Detective Smithers said. "Martin Simon."

"The kid from the dealership?" Detective Johnson replied. He pulled out the business card from his pocket. "He's barely linked to one case. Likely another coincidence and a dead end."

"It only takes one mistake for a killer to get caught sometimes," Agent Jansen added. "Shame. Dealership owner said the kid was going places. He was the new sales manager and had a keen ability to suss out the best of the new recruits."

"Hardly a poor judge of character," Detective Johnson replied. "If it's him, he's good. I never suspected he was lying. Maybe he was just being modest?"

"Call came in anonymously about an hour ago, but they said it sounded like an older Hispanic man," Detective Smithers said.

"Like from the video," Detective Johnson said as he stood up. "Maybe this is just the break we've been looking for, as unlikely as it might be."

Martin walked calmly through the abandoned building. He noted shafts of light stabbing the air from broken windows, illuminating floating dust, a broken concrete floor, and rusted remnants of bolts that had anchored large industrial equipment many years in the past. The lower floor was flanked on either side by empty offices, some with doors still in their frames. As Martin cleared them, he noted remnants of industrial bolts on their floors as well. Some of these rooms may have been some kind of workshop for refining tools or equipment. It all fell into the industrial category–maybe some kind of machining shop.

The center of the building was an open atrium. Martin glanced up at the other floors lined with hallways adorned with open walls to view the atrium from above. It was the perfect layout to ambush someone from above with a long-range weapon. Martin suddenly wished he had a helmet and some Kevlar.

Martin listened for any movement, but the constant whistling from the warm Santa Ana winds blowing through the broken windows gave a constant audio feedback of static to Martin's ears. He glanced from side to side as he followed the line of offices to the right.

In the middle of the building, one office sported a hammer hanging from twine in the center of the room. Martin entered the room cautiously, but the only thing of note was the tool hanging there.

"I've been waiting for you," a voice echoed in the atrium from somewhere in the building.

Martin walked to the office doorway and poked his head out, glancing up into the atrium. "Where are you?"

Martin called out. Even as he did so, he heard his own voice echo throughout the old building. Narrowing down the location of his target was going to be tricky.

"I would be foolish to show myself so quickly to a dangerous man like you," Hiram responded from an unknown spot in the building. The other man's voice bounced through the atrium. Martin squinted as he listened to the response, but between the constant wind and the echo in the building, he couldn't pinpoint the source.

"What do you want?" Martin shouted out again. He looked around and spotted a stairwell at the far end of the building that had a door hanging halfway off its hinges. He slowly made his way in that direction.

"Why, to give you your just reward for your murdering ways, of course. Now, the police have your Handyman body count at six; I'm guessing the real number is double that or more, perhaps in the neighborhood of twenty?" Hiram asked.

Martin stopped and listened closely as the man spoke. It seemed like his voice came from everywhere. He wondered if his quarry was even in the building. He could have wired the place with speakers. Martin realized he might be recorded by the mysterious stranger and frowned. He had to choose his words carefully.

"Hypothetically, that kind of killer could be closer to a count of fifty-four," Martin replied, though his only actual interest was in keeping his opponent talking so he could narrow down his location faster. He decided clearing the first floor might be best. He hurried to the other side of the building and began clearing the offices there quickly.

"My, my, you've been busy. But that count doesn't include the school, does it?"

Martin stopped dead in his tracks and stared up at the atrium ceiling, looking for telltale shadows, anything to indicate movement.

"I don't know what you're talking about," Martin responded as he walked out into the middle of the building and examined the second floor. Involuntarily, he spoke through clenched teeth. He forced himself to relax.

"Now, let's take a trip down memory lane Martin... oh, I'm sorry, you were Juan Vexler then, weren't you?"

Martin clenched his fists and took in a deep breath. *Who the fuck is this guy?*

"Look, I don't know what kind of drugs you're on, pal, but my name is Martin!" Martin let the emotion spill out in that exclamation and then took a moment to re-center himself.

"Martin was one of your classmates who died when you blew up the school with everyone in it. Nasty business, that. Lucky for you, there weren't any close family members left to scrutinize your identity."

Martin approached the lone closed door on the first floor and slowly turned the handle. He flung open the door, but it was similarly empty except for a screwdriver hanging from twine in the center of the room.

"Cute," Martin muttered. He stepped into the room just to make sure, but quickly exited. His mind traveled back to the school. The fire, the explosions from the gas line and seeing young Martin Simon's body burning in the hallway were still vivid in his memory. He wrinkled his nose as he remembered the smell of burning flesh. Juan Vexler swapped spots with the dead Martin that day. He tossed a few of his own personal items near Martin's dead body, including the fire starting tools he'd used that day. The police had rightfully suspected Juan of the crime, but failed to get the right body.

"You seem to know a lot about me," Martin shouted at the empty atrium. "But I don't remember you."

"We've never met, but you remember my granddaughter Maria, don't you? Otherwise, you wouldn't have come back to where you killed her trying to find me. She was the only thing keeping me from going over the edge," Hiram said, sounding properly sad at her passing.

"I'm sorry for your loss," Martin replied

"No, you aren't," Hiram said with a chuckle. "At least not yet."

"What?" Martin asked. A loud clang near the front door caught Martin's attention and he ran there. It was just the wind catching the front door. He closed it carefully to secure it better.

"I have gone back to my occult roots. A little voodoo, a little *Santeria*, a pinch of satanic rites and a drop of witchcraft all wrapped up in a fine gypsy curse. I even used some techniques I gleaned from the Book Of The Dead," Hiram said as Martin walked with purpose toward the stairwell at the other far end of the building.

"Sounds like you've gone to a lot of trouble for nothing," Martin said.

"In the two years since you took my *nieta*, I have planned my revenge. You're going to hell, Martin. Only, it will happen before you die."

"Sure, old man. Whatever," Martin replied as he passed the office with the hammer hanging in it.

"Your victims will come back to see you. All of them. Dead, but undead. You will have your final reckoning—your undead reckoning," Hiram stated.

Martin reached the stairwell and suddenly grabbed the back of his neck. "Ow!" Martin hollered. He turned around quickly and looked around the building, but saw nothing.

"Just needed a fresh blood sample for the spell. It won't be the last blood you spill," Hiram said. His voice sounded muted, like he'd turned away from the atrium or whatever he might have been speaking into.

"Yeah, I'm going to spill some of yours when I find you!" Martin hollered into the empty room.

"All in good time, Martin," Hiram said. "First, we'll set it all in motion, so you pay the price for killing what remained of my family."

There was a flash of light from near the center of the left side of the second floor. Martin turned into the stairwell and dashed up the stairs. "Gotcha!" Martin hissed.

Martin entered a room on the second floor just in time to see Hiram drop a handful of items into the flames of a bonfire. The fire crackled and flashed. "Now your account is due," Hiram said as he turned to face Martin.

"So is yours, old man," Martin replied as he stepped forward. He pulled one of his knives out and stabbed Hiram in the chest, piercing his heart. Hiram laughed for a moment and then fell to the floor, dead. The bonfire changed color to an icy blue.

"Nice spell," Martin said to Hiram's body. "Is the fire lit by eternal farts now?"

The flames flashed again and a wave of blue fire shot out in an ever-expanding circle at lightning speed. Martin jumped as it passed through him, but the weird light show appeared to have no effect on him.

Down the hillside from the road sign Martin passed earlier, a blue glow lit up a female corpse nestled in dry brush.

In the city morgue miles away, two corpses missing their right arms laid out on autopsy tables flashed with an eerie blue light.

A dozen grave markers in a cemetery glowed blue. Across the southwestern landscape for hundreds of miles, flashes of blue popped into existence for a brief moment and then faded away.

"Great fireworks show, old man. Maybe you'll get an anonymous high-five on your headstone," Martin said and laughed. He stepped up to Hiram and reached for his right arm, but hesitated. *Maybe this one should remain anonymous. The old codger really didn't do anything to warrant a grisly memorial.*

Martin looked around and found a piece of fishing line with a tiny, sharp dart tied at the end. It lay next to a blow dart weapon. He picked up the dart and examined it. He cast a glance at the blow dart weapon and kicked it into the fire. The glossy finish on the weapon must have been some kind of flammable varnish because it caught fire quickly and flared up. Martin rolled the rest of the fishing line up in his hand and took one last look at Hiram. He shook his head, walked away from Hiram and headed back to the stairwell.

Hiram's body briefly glowed with the blue light. The bonfire burned a bright blue for a moment and then returned to a normal yellow orange flame. Hiram's hand twitched against the cold cement floor.

The female corpse on the hill side stood up unsteadily and reached a left hand over to the rocks for stability. She climbed the rocky canyon wall toward the road sign. As she made her way up, she made a diagonal angle across the surface, edging incrementally closer to Martin's location even though he was miles away.

The two corpses on the autopsy tables sat up. They both swiveled their legs over the right side of the table and stepped down onto the cold tile floor. Small dirt clods, leaves, and chunks of congealed body fluid fell to the floor underneath them as they walked toward the exit.

The ground at the cemetery appeared to bubble as hands in various states of decay broke the surface. Some of the hands were little more than skeletal.

Martin got to his car, still holding the bloody knife, the needle-like dart and fishing line. He popped open the trunk with his free hand, pulled out a coffee can, some lighter fluid and bleach wipes. The wipes he used to wiped off the knife before placing any used wipes in the can. After placing the tiny dart and line inside, he pulled off the gloves and deposited them in the can as well. With a generous amount of lighter fluid squirted in the can, the contents of the can lit up easily using the long-handled barbecue lighter.

He ran the open flame along the length of the knife to further remove any traces from the blade and hilt. After scrutinizing it, he used another wipe to clean off any soot. The wipe joined the other combustibles in the burning can and he put the knife back in the leather case. One quick inspection of the other knives from his vest proved them clean, and he put them back in the case as well. Finally, he removed the vest and looked at it for any trace of blood from Hiram that might've splashed on it. While he couldn't find any, he knew a meticulous cleaning was in order when he got back to his base of operations. To reduce any cross contamination, he wrapped the vest in a garbage bag, then put the vest and case back in the satchel in the trunk.

He pulled a paper towel from the trunk and found a loose stick in the undergrowth near the parking area. Using the towel as a handle, he stirred the coffee can to ensure everything burned to ashes. It was all broken down except for the small dart. He walked over to the undergrowth and scattered the ashes on the bushes there. It would blend in with the ash from the frequent wild fires in the area. He doubted the dart, now sterilized by fire, would provide any relevant DNA evidence connecting him to the site. Just the same, he used his shirt to pick up the needle and embedded it into the stick. He tossed the stick far away into the brush down the hillside and put the coffee can back in the trunk with the carefully folded paper towel.

When he stopped on the shoulder on the other side of the road just across from the parking lot, he retrieved a small rake from the trunk. Returning to the parking lot, he carefully scraped away any shoe or tire imprints from the building all the way to the road. After a half hour's worth of work, he looked the area over and nodded.

When he returned to the asphalt surface, he tapped loose dirt off the rake onto the road surface between the parking area and the shoulder where he parked. A quick spray of water from a bottle in the trunk and the rake was clean. He used the paper towel to dry it off before setting the rake back in the trunk and repeated the process with his shoes. Finally, he folded the paper towel up and set it in the coffee can. Checking his surroundings as he closed the trunk, he noticed nothing but dusk approaching. There was no police activity or anyone on the road that he would have to track down. It couldn't have been a more simple elimination of a witness.

Yet...

Martin stared at the building he left Hiram in for a few seconds and frowned. It was definitely the weirdest experience of his life. He didn't know what to make of the unusual theatrical production.

What did you even have to gain from this nonsense, old man? Maybe you were just crazy. But then, aren't we all?

Martin started up the car and drove away. His mind reviewed the circumstances of his out of character kill. He was sure just leaving the body there would annoy him to no end. He always disposed of the body. Surely, if the police connected the old man to the video, they would draw the conclusion that the Handyman killer was behind his demise. Had that been the point all along?

Did he just want to draw me out and hope I made a mistake? Did I make a mistake?

He reviewed every step in his mind, but it was a jumble of standard procedures and unique movements and activities. Was there something he'd overlooked in pursuit of this singular eyewitness to his crimes? The permutations were endless. It vexed him to not have all the answers, and he feared he'd never find them.

CHAPTER 4

Dinesh stepped off the elevator and closed the case file for one of the dead bodies in the morgue. The John Doe was a little less decomposed than the Jane Doe, but it would still be a long night making measurements, pulling DNA samples and getting dental x-rays to identify them. At least they weren't burned. Dinesh hated the crispy ones.

He turned the corner, heading toward the morgue, and his jaw dropped open. The two corpses that had been on his autopsy tables were now ambling toward him. For a moment, he froze in shock. Fear took over and he ran for the elevator.

Dinesh got to the elevator and pressed the button. The elevator had already gone up, so he had to wait for it to come back down. He turned to go back toward the stairs, but the two zombies had already passed that door, blocking his exit. Dinesh pressed the call button again and again as the two animated corpses stepped closer to him, silent except for the shuffling of their feet on the linoleum hallway floor.

Dinesh whimpered as he looked at them. The difference in their state of decomposition was less obvious from this standpoint. Both corpses were exposed to the elements, animals and insects for months. Most of their flesh was gone and the clothes barely hung onto their skeletons. The man still wore a dress shirt and tie, though both were so discolored Dinesh couldn't tell what color they'd been originally. Pants were still bound by a belt and somehow hung to the hip bones of the deceased male. The woman wore a simple flower dress that looked like it had been in a smoker's home for years. Dinesh realized the particular discoloration was just from bodily fluids and decayed flesh, parts of which still dropped from somewhere inside the dress to the floor, leaving a trail behind her like breadcrumbs marking her passage.

The details and his analysis were just a jumble is his mind of pure panic as the duo got closer to him. There was a ding as the elevator arrived and the doors slid open behind Dinesh. He fell backward into the elevator. He frantically clawed at the Close button for the elevator doors and pushed it repeatedly, but the zombies walked into the cab before he could get it closed. Dinesh screamed and passed out.

The two zombies looked down at Dinesh briefly before turning around to face the doors as they closed. The deceased woman was closer to the buttons, so she pressed to the first floor call button a few times. Her decayed finger slid off the smooth surface several times before she just slammed the button with her skeletal fist. As the elevator rose to smooth jazzy music playing overhead, the zombies looked at each other and nodded, even though neither of them had eyeballs in their sockets.

With a clunky slide, the elevator doors opened on the first floor and the zombies stepped out. People happening by screamed in panic and ran from the zombies. The zombies appeared no more interested in the fleeing hospital employees than they'd been in the morgue worker passed out on the floor of the elevator.

Dinesh's eyes fluttered open. As he listened to the soft jazz playing overhead, he watched the zombies walk away from him. The elevator doors slowly closed and they disappeared. His mind couldn't put the facts of the situation together in any logical combination, and he passed out again.

The zombies continued their inexorable path to the side exit of the building and walked out.

Martin tapped his fingers on the steering wheel nervously. His mind repeated the old man's words and something bugged him about it.

Victims would come back. His account had become due.

Martin nodded at the last part. It was only a matter of time before his string of murders caught up to him, regardless of how careful he was. He turned on the radio. He wondered if the old man had stacked the deck against him and revealed what he knew already. Had the old bastard revealed the location of more of his kills, something that could nail down a pattern of behavior? Had the authorities already put it together? Would they be looking for Martin? The old man knew way more about Martin than he thought possible.

His mind traveled back to the events before the school exploded in flame, killing everyone but him inside. The timing of the real Martin being between foster homes had been key; that and they were similar enough to be brothers. Over time, a slow and sloppy social worker allowed him to put all his own information, pictures and pertinent data in Martin's file. As far as the authorities were concerned, Juan Vexler died in the fire, joining his murdered parents in death-a murder suicide by all appearances. It was the only killing he regretted, but it had been a matter of survival.

Maybe the old man had just researched enough to put together a conjecture. That codger couldn't possibly have actual proof, no matter his apparent blackmail scheme.

He cocked his head at a person walking along the road ahead on the left. He drove past the person on the side of the road and they seemed to follow him as he passed. Just beyond the stranger on the side of the road, Martin saw the road sign marking the last resting place of the woman he killed months ago and dropped off the side of the mountain. His eyebrows slowly furrowed as he contemplated the situation.

That's gotta be kismet. I can put another body in the same location–should drive the police nuts if they happen upon it.

He made a u-turn and pulled up next to the sign. The headlights showed the woman walking toward him. She looked rough, like she'd been in a terrible car accident. It was hard to gauge in the glare of the headlights; the halogens lit up the subject just a little too much. Martin smiled.

Easy kill. Should take the edge off.

Martin got out of the car and ran around to the trunk. He opened it and pulled out a pair of surgical gloves, sliding them on quickly. He paused and looked into the trunk. This wasn't his modus operandi. He didn't just kill random people. He sighed. This person was just a victim of running out of gas, or maybe she'd been in a car accident. She'd done nothing to deserve his wrath. He would not kill another innocent. Well, not someone who wasn't a threat somehow, even to his admittedly twisted definition of what constituted a threat. He pulled the gloves off and put them back in the trunk.

If I can help her anonymously, she can just get home safe. No harm done.

He stepped forward with the car behind him and watched the woman walking toward him with an odd shuffle.

"Hey, did you run out of gas or something? You need some help?" Martin asked.

As she got closer, and passed in and out of the shadow he cast in the headlights, he noticed her skin appeared mottled and rotten.

"What the hell?" he murmured.

The woman launched herself at Martin, left hand grabbing at him as he dodged out of the way. Now she was between him and the car. "You killed me," Rebecca said, her voice a raspy gurgle.

"Right... interesting night for a joke. Are you cosplaying or something?" Martin laughed, but she surprised him with her speed when she lunged at him and grabbed his throat with her left hand. Her shirt rose up, drawing his eyes down to her abdomen, which was largely missing. Bits of dirt and tumbleweed fell out of the ragged cavity scavengers and insects had carved out of her stomach.

Just before Martin hit her in the face, he noticed a small jade quarter moon pendant partially covered by dirt and grime glistening in the headlights. As some of the skin sloughed off her skull, sticking to his knuckles, he tried to place the pendant in his memory. It eluded him, which frustrated him more than battling what appeared to be a corpse.

The blow from his fist pushed hair caked with mud and

dried bodily fluids to the side. For the first time, Martin saw most of her face had rotted away and there were no eyeballs in the sockets. He struggled to push out a scream as he grabbed at the powerful hand grasping his throat.

In a panic, he kicked at her chest and she fell backward. Her left arm separated from her body as the hand still held firm around his throat, tightening and cutting off his oxygen.

As Rebecca struggled to stand up with no arms to assist her recently animated body, Martin grabbed the fingers of the undead hand and pried them from apart, breaking several of the bony and slimy fingers. He threw the severed arm at Rebecca and she tried to catch it with the stump of her missing right arm.

"Your other hand..." Martin said with a gulp as he massaged his throat. The memory of the pendant flooded back to him. It had been on the neck of the woman he'd tossed off the side.

"You cut it off before you killed me, don't you remember?" Rebecca replied. She ran at him. Martin was ready for her speed this time; he dodged her and ran back to his car. He opened the door and watched Rebecca's shuffling corpse turn around.

"That was three months ago!" he shouted.

"I've been waiting to kill you back!" she screeched and ran at the car.

Martin climbed in and started the car. He quickly rolled up his window before she collided with it, banging on the tempered glass with her rotted torso and skull, leaving a trail of slime and dirt behind with each impact. Martin stomped on the accelerator and tore off down the road, running over

Rebecca's wriggling left arm, crushing the elbow joint. The arm continued to wiggle and squirm.

Martin went about a half mile down the road and slowly turned the car around. He reached up to his throat and touched it. It hurt and, when he looked at his hand as he drew it away, he found it stained with his own blood. Hiram's words popped into his mind.

It won't be the last blood you spill.

He turned on the high beams and, at the edge of their reach, he saw Rebecca headed toward him in a staggered run.

"Let's see you come after me when you're in pieces, bitch!" Martin growled and pressed his foot on the accelerator again, racing toward the undead woman. As Martin got closer, he gunned the engine and drove right through her, splattering goo and flesh pieces all over his car and the road. He slammed on his brakes and little pieces of Rebecca rolled back down his windshield and lay on the hood of his car. The bigger bits still pulsated and undulated on the maroon finish.

"What the hell is going on?" Martin whispered as he his eyes got wider. Bits of flesh migrated up the hood toward him. He looked in the rear-view mirror behind him. The road glistened in the moonlight with soured body fluids and rotted flesh; some of it still moved on the asphalt surface.

"No fucking way," Martin muttered and raced down the road. The remaining chunks of flesh rolled up the windshield and disappeared behind him. With shaking fingers, he turned on the radio. Oingo Boingo's *It's a Dead Man's Party* came on the radio as part of the countdown to Halloween. He quickly turned the radio off.

CHAPTER 5

"We got anything new on this Martin guy?" Detective Johnson asked. He stood next to Detective Smithers, who busily typed on the keyboard, stopping every few moments to adjust something with his mouse.

"I've dug through every database I can access and there's nothing. He's squeaky clean," Detective Smithers said, shaking his head. "He doesn't even own a car."

"How does he get around?"

"He works at a dealership. They can check out their loaner vehicles, which he does regularly." Detective Smithers shrugged his shoulders.

"You spoke with the dealership owner but didn't tell him anything, right? We don't want to spook Martin if he shows up there."

"He's off work today," Detective Smithers said. "But I can't imagine it isn't raising some suspicions. At some point, his boss will suspect something is up. We're asking a lot of questions in excess of a normal casual query. At least he's cooperating."

Agent Jensen walked up and smiled at the detectives. "I think we've got something," he said and waved them to follow him to the conference room. Inside the conference room, two more agents sat at the table working at laptops. Agent Jensen pointed to the video displayed on the wall.

"We've done a deep dive on Martin and come up with an interesting history. He was the sole survivor of a fire at a middle school that was apparently set by a Juan Vexler after Juan killed his parents, well, his mother and stepfather. History of abuse in the Vexler household according to neighbors, but there was no record with local law enforcement or CPS. That likely led Juan to set the fire, but otherwise, it's not relevant.

However, Martin rolled through a set of foster homes before and after the fire. As foster homes are not always the most nurturing of environments, he had some friction with a few of the foster families, including one where the foster father had an accident with a power tool in the garage and lost use of his right arm. Permanent nerve damage. He evidently abused kids when he had use of the right arm, but those reports died off after the accident."

"And did the kid do it?" Detective Johnson asked.

"Well, the authorities investigated because the man blamed Martin, who denied any responsibility. With the foster father's history of blaming his foster kids for criminal activities, including shoplifting, which it was later discovered the foster father had done himself, the police discounted his story and never pursued it. Martin moved onto another foster home and there was never any more trouble until he graduated high school."

"What happened after high school?"

"Nothing of note. Pretty bland existence in and out of community college doing odd jobs until he landed at the dealership."

"Doesn't sound like much of a profile. Maybe I'm missing the connection? Is it the incident with the foster father?" Detective Smithers folded his arms and cocked his head.

"It's the incredible lack of anything," the agent sitting in front of one laptop said.

"This is Agent Laura Mendoza," Agent Jensen explained as he nodded to the agent who had just spoken. "One of our best and brightest."

"There's very little in the way of purchases outside of home furnishings, clothing and cleaning supplies," Agent Mendoza continued. "An excessively large amount of cleaning supplies."

"Well," Detective Johnson said. "Martin's boss described Martin as very meticulous. Being a clean freak doesn't equate to being a murderer and a single instance of someone's arm getting mangled is a stretch."

"So, his purchase history and general history are clean. Super clean," Agent Mendoza said. "Too clean."

"Too clean?" Detective Smithers asked.

"He's a ghost," Agent Mendoza said. "There's nothing to suggest he has hobbies or interests outside of eating at home and working. There's no trail of his life anywhere outside of those two locations and the grocery store."

"He's boring and clean, but….." Detective Johnson shrugged his shoulders.

"Why get the cars from the dealership if you're never going anywhere?" Agent Jensen interjected.

"It didn't look like there was a lot of mileage on the cars after he turned them in," Detective Smithers noted as he stood up and stretched his back.

"Nothing out of the ordinary. Certainly nothing to suggest using the loaner vehicles to dispose of the bodies. There's literally no paper trail of him going outside the triangle of home, dealership and store."

"All cash purchases are unusual," Detective Smithers said. "But not impossible. Another quirk perhaps."

"Where is he now?" Agent Mendoza asked.

"Well, we don't know," Detective Johnson replied. "We have a unit watching his apartment. You think he's grocery shopping?"

"We think he makes a lot of money at the dealership, in the high six figures, and we don't see where that money has gone. It's not in his accounts. That money is in the wind. We think he has other accounts under assumed names, maybe even in crypto. He's a ghost or, at the very least, his financial activities mirror those of a ghost agent."

"So, the absence of evidence is the actual evidence," Detective Smithers surmised. "Where does that leave us?"

"With a lot of questions, but not a lot of answers," Agent Jensen replied. "But it also tells us there's more to Martin Simon than meets the eye. This is where the hunt gets interesting."

Martin pulled into the manual car wash bay and got out of the car. The bits of debris coating his car caused him to curse silently as he walked to the pay station and looked at the machine.

"Fuck," he said. It only accepted credit cards. Martin looked around and sighed. He'd have to retire this card after today; there was too much chance of a forensic connection.

After he swiped the credit card from one of his many dummy accounts, the water trickled out of the hose. He nicked the edge of the card surface so he could easily identify it for disposal later and put it back in his wallet. The funds in that account would have to be scrubbed–all for a car wash. He clenched his teeth as he returned the wallet to his back pocket.

Martin cleaned the surface grime off the car. Chunks of Rebecca, still wriggling with an undead life of their own, fell off the car and went down the drain. Larger bits flopped around in the water inside the drain. Switching the wand to soap, Martin covered the car in suds, then scrubbed with the brush next, getting every surface, including the tires. Finally, he rinsed off the vehicle and stood back. He debated using the car wash wax, but knew it was horribly substandard and would do more harm than good. The car had earned a proper shine when he got to his warehouse. The mirrors, though, could use a towel if nothing else. Hanging up the car wash wand, he went behind the car and popped open the trunk. Scraping footsteps behind him made him casually flipped open his satchel. Inside the case, his hand came to rest on one of the knife handles.

"Hey, *ese*. You don't look like you're from around here," said a Hispanic voice behind him.

"Yeah, *ese*, you lost? He looks like he's lost, Hector," said a second voice with a deeper accent.

Martin half turned to them, keeping his hand on the knife hilt. He took them in quickly, noting the wife beater shirts and low hung jeans, but no obvious gang colors. They weren't Crips or Bloods, but more likely affiliated with a smaller outlier gang or perhaps just random street thugs with no gang affiliation. That meant they were more than likely running solo and didn't have any backup if things went bad. Things were about to go bad.

"I just pulled in to wash my car. I don't want any trouble," Martin said as he cocked his head politely toward them, knowing it was pointless as the two men adjusted their feet in a pre-attack stance.

"No trouble here, right, Antonio?" Hector said with a glance at his partner.

"Yeah," Antonio replied with a chuckle. "No trouble as long as you pay us a parking fee for parking your car here in our territory."

They used their names. They're either stupid or don't plan on letting me live through this to make a statement.

Martin slid the knife out of the case, keeping it just out of view inside the bag. "Great. How much is that gonna cost?" Martin asked.

"Just your car keys, man," Hector said with a smile as he pulled out a switchblade. Antonio pulled out a matching piece with a rabbit's foot dangling from the hilt. Dried blood matted the surface of the good luck charm.

They took one step toward Martin, but weren't expecting the resistance or speed with which their prey reacted. The serial killer swung the large knife in a precise arc, cutting Antonio's throat and nicking Hector's outstretched hand holding the switchblade. Antonio immediately dropped his weapon and clutched his throat as spurting blood spit up into the surrounding air. While Hector screamed in pain at the slice in his hand, Martin plunged the knife deep into Hector's chest, carving a hole so big in the thug's heart he nearly cleaved it in two. Hector clutched at his chest as he went to his knees and fell on his face, gasping for breath just for a few moments before he stopped moving altogether.

Martin walked over to the still spraying car wash wand and rinsed off the knife. Quickly drying the blade off on his pants, he made a mental note to dispose of his clothing and give the knives a proper cleaning again when he got home. In a well-practiced motion, he returned the knife to the satchel and closed the trunk. Antonio gave his last gasp and died. Martin looked at the two men and shook his head. He stepped toward the driver's side door when he heard movement behind him. Whirling around, his jaw dropped as both men got to their feet unsteadily. They looked at him and he noticed their eyes clouded over with a white film accompanied by a familiar blue light.

"Looks like we're gonna need something more as payment after all," Hector said. Next to him, Antonio tried to speak, but it came out as a gurgle, since Martin's attack bisected his vocal cords.

"No," Martin said, pointing at them as they took a hesitant step forward. "No! When I kill something, it's supposed to stay dead!"

Martin pulled the car door opened and shut it quickly. As he started the car, the undead gang members jumped on his hood and smacked their hands on his windshield. Martin put the car in reverse and burned rubber out of the car wash bay, throwing Hector off the hood. Antonio busted through the windshield and grabbed at Martin.

Martin drove forward wildly, trying to throw Antonio off. Finally, he slammed on the brakes. Antonio lost his hold on Martin and caught the edge of the hood. Martin put the car in reverse again and screamed back down the street, causing Antonio to lose his grip and fly off the car. He rolled after the car for a while, limbs flailing wildly.

Hector burst through the driver's side window, latching onto Martin's shoulder with his teeth. Martin screamed in pain and put the car in a donut spin, trying to dislodge Hector from his painful grip. Hector held onto the door with his hands and kept his teeth firmly implanted in Martin's shoulder.

Martin looked to the street ahead of him and spotted a telephone pole unobstructed by anything else on his side of the car. He drove forward at full speed and angled it so it would collide with Hector's body dangling outside the car door. The impact dislodged Hector from Martin's shoulder, but also severed Hector's body from his head. Hector's head fell into the back seat while his body lay inert next to the cracked telephone pole.

"Sick bastard!" Hector's disembodied head chided him. "Guess all you wanted was a little head! Ha ha ha!"

Martin stopped the car and looked in the back seat. Hector licked his lips at him and wiggled his eyebrows. Martin watched in the mirror as Hector's body got up a few hundred feet behind the car and held onto the cracked telephone pole for balance. He turned to look in front of the car just in time to see Antonio stumble forward into an open manhole and disappear from sight.

Martin sighed and turned back around. He pushed the broken windshield out from in front of him and then drove forward. Hector's laughter filled the night air.

CHAPTER 6

*M*artin pulled up on a hillside overlooking his apartment and scanned the street below. A police cruiser sat within sight of his front door. As Martin watched, another police cruiser appeared at the end of the street with its lights on. It passed the other cruiser but didn't stop.

"Oh, pretty lights!" Hector chimed in from the back seat. "Hey piggies, over here! I fucked your piggy momma! Ha ha ha!"

"Holy shit," Martin muttered and drove away. "Fuckin' old man was a rat too."

Martin pulled up to a red light and stopped. He looked at Hector's head sitting in the back seat, staring back at him with a big grin. "How are you still alive?" Martin asked.

"I don't know, *ese*," Hector responded. "This is your freak show, not mine."

"I don't like it," Martin muttered.

"Yeah?" Hector responded. "Well, I don't like being dead, but here we are!"

"Shut up," Martin said as the light turned green. He turned onto the freeway on-ramp and Hector's head slid into the door with a wet thud.

"You keep knocking, but there's no 'body' home! Get it?" Hector shouted.

Martin clenched his teeth and kept driving. The talking head in the back seat was the least of his worries. His car was a mess and that weighed heavily on his mind. His urge to stop again and hit another car wash pounded his sanity like a sledgehammer. He couldn't concentrate on trying to figure out what was going on. The car being such a wreck jumbled everything in his mind. There was a remnant of blood on his jeans. The knife required cleaning and sterilizing. A thousand details about the car's condition kept rolling through his mind from the dents on the hood and fenders to the shattered windshield. At least the wind coming in through the missing windshield almost drowned out Hector's singing.

He watched his speed as he drove. There was no need to attract undo attention beyond his slightly damaged and messy car. The state registration led to an alias; there was no hint that they'd broken into that digital web of detours and dead ends he'd devised. Although, given what the old man had dug up on him, he doubted anything could remain irretrievably lost, no matter how well he'd buried it.

He watched the sidewalks for anything weird. Every once in a while, he turned to look in the back seat at the disembodied head riding along with him. With the dead coming back to life and the cops hot on his trail, his mind was foggier than ever. Not much of it made any sense.

The surreptitious appearance of a familiar gas station sign reminded him of a past kill and, while he normally reveled in reliving those moments of vengeance, it brought him little solace now. He took an on-ramp to another highway and took a deep breath. He needed some distance from the police staking out his home. They wouldn't find much there if they got a search warrant. They'd need to tear up the cupboards to find his spare set of weapons, which wouldn't give them anything concrete for a case against him. Given what they could easily find on Martin, he doubted they'd have probable cause to get a judge to sign off on that kind of intrusion into his apartment. There simply wasn't anything easy to find.

"Highway to hell," Hector began singing in the back seat. Martin frowned and looked back at the head for a moment. The surreal moment returned his attention to his current circumstances.

"Dead, but undead," Martin whispered. "That's crazy."

Marla Vincenzo held the leash for her Chihuahua, Francisco. The little dog sniffed the brick wall of the cemetery and lifted his leg to leave a small sample of urine trickling down the faded brick, darkening its surface. Marla sighed. Her little pet had been doing this for this last hour and seemed to have an infinite bladder. She really didn't understand where all the pee came from.

Suddenly, Francisco stiffened and his ears perked up. She saw his little nose twitch as he sniffed the air. He turned to the wall and started barking furiously at it, backing away, and tugging with fury at the leash. Marla frowned as her little canine tugged her arm in a futile effort. She reached down to pick him up, but he snapped at her. She jumped and shrieked. Francisco never snapped at her, just at all her boyfriends.

Finally, she turned toward the wall to see if she could see what had Francisco in a tizzy. That was when an arm reached out of the darkness and grabbed onto the top of the four foot tall wall. In the dim light from the street lamps, the hand that grasped at the top of the bricks seemed partially rotted away. Maria screamed and ran away from the wall in the direction Francisco had been tugging. Francisco joined in her frantic flight from the cemetery wall.

Like a slow moving tidal wave, bodies crawled over the wall and plopped down on the other side. They picked themselves up and continued down the street, angling across it, heading to the same destination.

Milo Dershowitz rubbed his eyes as he climbed the canyon road. It had been a long twelve-hour shift; he was looking forward to a few days off. The medical resident had gotten together with five other residents and pooled their resources for a swanky but cramped place up in the hills overlooking Los Angeles. One of his roommates, Ellen Tervis, snoozed away in the back seat.

She woke up instantly when Milo came around a corner and slammed on his brakes. They watched several people in the road ahead of them stumble their way across from one side to the other. They crawled up from the canyon side of the road, made their way across, and began climbing up the other side. Milo put on the hazard lights and got out of the car to see if he could help.

Ellen groaned as she unbuckled and joined Milo outside the car. If someone was in trouble medically, it was their obligation to help them. She fervently wished the other four residents were in the same car, but they were still miles behind. The two of them had gotten off earlier than the sixteen hours they were normally on and she was so looking forward to the extra sleep, but the Hippocratic oath they'd taken compelled them to ignore their exhaustion. They had to do the right thing.

As Ellen got out of the car, she saw Milo walk up to the people climbing the canyon wall and speak, but none of them responded. He put his hand up and waved his hand in front of the person's face, but they didn't respond. His other hand was in front of his own face. He turned around and Ellen saw Milo pinching his nostrils shut. He walked back to the car.

"What's happening?" Ellen asked. "Should I get one of our medical bags from the trunk?"

Milo released his nostrils and shook his head. He went around to the passenger side of the car and retrieved a flashlight from the glove compartment. He turned to Ellen.

"You've got to see this, but you probably should plug your nose," Milo said and walked back toward the people trying to climb. Ellen joined him and grabbed her nose as they got closer.

"What the hell?" Ellen said in a nasally rasp.

Milo shined the flashlight on the people and both medical residents could see these walking dead were in various states of decay. There were four of them attempting to scale the canyon wall heading back toward Los Angeles. They walked around the climbers and noted all of them had their right hand and forearm removed. Milo walked over to the other side of the road and looked down into the canyon. He spotted at least two more figures trying to scale the rocky wall below.

"What do we do?" Ellen asked. The undead didn't approach the two of them or even acknowledge their presence.

"Well, I can't render medical assistance to..." Milo

pointed at the closet climber. "That. I say we call nine-one-one and tell them there are some people who appear to be injured here in the canyon and wait for the authorities to arrive."

"Wait? How long will that take?" Ellen asked as she yawned. Milo yawned as well.

"Good point. As interesting as it is to see real life zombies, I don't want to endure whatever black ops FBI agents would do to us in interrogations. Let's call in a car accident, give the mile marker and tell them to send emergency personnel. They can figure it out from there."

Milo got in the car. Ellen hesitated. She looked at the climbers attempting to scale the wall in futility, not just because it was a hard wall to climb, but also because climbing canyon walls was easier if you weren't missing limbs. She sighed and climbed back into the car. Milo picked up his phone, but Ellen pushed it down.

"I'd rather sleep," she said. "Let someone else make an emergency call about zombies. That is well outside our job description."

Milo started the car up and drove carefully around the zombies and continued on his way. Ellen lay back down and easily closed her eyes.

Even with the incessant chatter from the disembodied head in the back seat, Martin was able to concentrate on the street signs over the intervening hour and find his exit. After a few turns in an industrial area of the city, Martin arrived at a row of warehouse buildings. He scanned the area for any police activity. There wasn't even a spot of transient activity that he sometimes witnessed down here. Everything seemed clear.

He traveled along the loading docks until he reached a

door halfway down the building and stopped the car. He turned the car off and listened carefully.

"Oh, how romantic!" Hector exclaimed from the back seat. "There's nothing I want more than to sit with you here in the dark. Why don't you pull me close for a cuddle?"

Martin groaned and got out of the car. He opened the back door and grabbed Hector by the hair, removing him from the back seat.

"Hair we go!" Hector babbled then laughed.

Martin clenched his jaw as he ascended the stairs and worked the combination padlock on the door with one hand. He walked into the building and the motion sensor lights came on, immediately illuminating the large warehouse. Along the back wall there was a workbench lined with knives and various construction tools mounted on wall hooks that could easily be employed for dismembering bodies. He tossed Hector's head onto the workbench and walked over to a utility sink with a large basin.

"Hey, what are we doing here, Rico Suave?" Hector said as his head rolled to lie on its side. Martin turned the water on and washed his hands.

"We're going to find out what it takes to shut you up," Martin said as he dried his hands and grabbed a large knife from another wall lined with tools and cutting instruments.

"Oh, I can tell you. Come over here and I'll whisper it in your ear," Hector said.

"So you can bite my ear off? I don't think so," Martin replied. He opened a drawer and pulled out a pair of blue surgical gloves. He slid them on quickly and picked the knife back up.

"Aw, man. Who told you?" Hector crowed. "It was

supposed to be a secret. Is it my fault I like white meat?"

Martin grabbed Hector's head by the hair again and set it upright. He raised the knife and plunged down into the top of Hector's skull. Hector screamed and then laughed.

"That tickles, *ese!*" Hector shouted.

Martin held the skull still with one hand as he pulled the knife out with the other. He walked back to the sink, tossed the knife into it and washed the gloves off in the sink. A quick search of a storage cabinet revealed a huge plastic jar, which he filled up with water from the sink. He set the jar next to the disembodied head.

"Hey wait, man!" Hector screamed as his eyes got wide. "I can't swim!"

Martin grabbed Hector's head by the hair again and lowered it into the water. Even as the talking head hit the bottom of the jar, Martin could tell it wouldn't do much good. Hector's mouth still moved as though he was talking and the eyes followed his every movement.

"Didn't exactly shut your mouth," Martin said to the jar. "But at least I can't hear you anymore."

Martin walked to a bathroom near the front of the warehouse, pulled off his shirt and put it in the trash can. He examined his shoulder and neck wounds. The shoulder wounds were pretty deep where Hector's teeth had pierced the flesh, but the neck abrasions and cuts seemed pretty superficial. The cabinet underneath the bathroom sink held a first aid kit he used to clean his wounds, suture the shoulder wounds and apply gauze and tape to them. Only two of the cuts on his neck were deep enough to warrant a small bandage on each; Martin surmised those were probably where most of the blood came from. Besides using antibiotic ointment, Martin popped a few pain pills and downed a sports drink. His shoulder really hurt and the surrounding bruising discolored his light brown skin.

When he finished his medical tasks, Martin cleaned the sink thoroughly until it was spotless and placed all the trash in the trash can. After some squirts from a bottle filled with a bleach solution designed to clean, sanitize, and destroy DNA, he placed all the supplies back under the sink, arranging everything perfectly spaced before he closed the cabinet door.

He retrieved the trash bag and walked to the rear wall of the warehouse where an industrial furnace he installed years ago lay dormant. He placed the bag inside, closed the door and turned the furnace on. Returning to the sink area, he noticed Hector mouthing something, but didn't really care what the undead head was spouting. A generous amount of bleach solution splashed over the knife and sink as he thoroughly cleaned and sterilized the sink and the area around Hector's jar.

Martin squinted at Hector and figured out he chanted 'Mister Clean' over and over. He raised an eyebrow at the floating head. He glanced around the room and felt like all surfaces were bright, shining, and free of DNA evidence. Martin disposed of all the cleaning rags and his gloves in the industrial furnace.

Next, Martin went into a front office and came back carrying a complete car windshield. He took this outside and leaned it against the loading dock. He returned to the warehouse and retrieved tools, additional car supplies, and a few buckets. Within thirty minutes, he removed the broken windshield and debris, cleaned the car interior, and set the new windshield in place.

He picked up the buckets full of debris and carried them back inside. He took a few minutes to deposit everything he pulled off the car in the furnace. After he completed this task, he stepped over to a refrigerator and pulled out a bottle of water. In the silence, he detected some kind of rhythmic pounding. He squinted his eyes and concentrated, but couldn't be sure it wasn't just the blood rushing through his own ears.

Freshly hydrated, he returned to the car with cleaning supplies and made the maroon sedan spotless again, banged out dents, buffed out scratches and applied paint repair compounds to them. He finally waxed the entire vehicle and stepped back to admire his handiwork. In the low lighting from the sparse lights in the warehouse complex, it was difficult to see the hard work Martin put into restoring his vehicle, but he knew his work was close to flawless. The morning sun might reveal a different scenario, but he felt he'd done all he could here tonight. He smiled and retrieved the supplies.

Martin walked into the warehouse and put everything back. He returned to the furnace and shut it down. After a few minutes, Martin noticed the weird repetitive thumping sound he thought had been in his head came from an area he hadn't visited since he entered the warehouse that night–a large walk-in freezer with a huge combination padlock on it.

Martin glanced at Hector's head inside the jar, staring back at him. He rubbed his eyes and shook his head. He walked by the jar back into the front office. Just inside the office door, there was a baseball bat with a handle wrapped in tape; he brought it with him to the freezer door. Setting the bat down, he opened the combination lock, popped the lock off the door and stuck it in his back pocket. A quick glance back at Hector revealed the undead head sported a huge grin on his submerged face.

Martin pulled the door open and took in the frozen forearms hanging on the walls, gyrating on their hooks trying to get loose. After frowning at their unexplained animation, he scanned the rest of the freezer but saw nothing out of the ordinary populating his trophy case.

His eyes lingered on each prize, remembering the kills as if they were yesterday. Each trophy represented an abusive person who met their timely end at his hands and his knife. There were mothers, fathers and some plain old hapless jerks out for a night's abuse. He felt sorry for none of them.

"But they shouldn't be moving," Martin whispered.

"It's a little unnerving, isn't it?" a voice said from behind him. Martin whirled around with his bat raised to strike. Hiram stood next to the sink and leaned against the counter. The old man looked pale with white, glossed over eyes like Martin had noticed with the two gang members he'd dispatched earlier. He glanced at Hector, who raised his eyebrows.

Martin slammed the freezer shut and advanced on Hiram, bat raised. Hiram held up his hands.

"Hey, I'm not one of the zombies trying to kill you. You should save that energy for the others," Hiram said as he pointed a thumb at Hector in the jar. Martin looked at Hector and then at the warehouse front door, standing wide open. He strode over to it, shut it and locked it.

Hiram strode over to the freezer and observed the door.

"Nice trophy case," Hiram said. "No dusting required."

Martin walked over to the sink and removed the long knife he'd used on Hector's disembodied head earlier. He set the bat down and ran at Hiram, who just stood there with a smirk on his face.

Martin plunged the knife into the hole already present in Hiram's bare chest, piercing his heart yet again. The knife went so deep the point pushed Hiram's suit coat out at the back. Hiram noted where the knife was sunk into his chest and then looked at Martin.

"Well, you're consistent. I'll give you that," Hiram said.

Martin shook his head as he slowly stepped back, pulling the long knife out of Hiram. The edge caught on Hiram's heart and it stuck to the knife. Part of Hiram's chest wall came away with the wriggling heart still stuck on the other side. Martin's eyes got wide. He reflexively dropped the knife, chunk of chest wall, heart and all, to the floor. He stared at the beating heart lying on the floor, skewered like a shish kabob. It pulsated slowly, glistening with the illumination from the bright overhead lights.

Hiram leaned down and grabbed the knife handle. With a flick of his wrist, he sent his heart sailing through the air, hitting a stunned Martin solid in the chest. Martin caught the wriggling heart by reflex and then dropped it, horrified.

"Thought we could have a heart to heart before you go," Hiram said with a grin.

"What are you?" Martin asked as he back away. He glanced at Hector–the disembodied head was literally rolling with laughter inside the jar.

"Well," Hiram began as he walked forward and picked

up his heart. "Thanks to you, I'm a zombie instead of a warrior fighting off the legions of undead coming after us. Well, coming after you now."

"What?"

"Sorry," Hiram said as he put his heart back in his chest and slid the chest wall back into place. Hiram looked down at his chest and pushed it around. The flesh held fast, but wiggled a bit. "Hmm, should wear a shirt to keep this all together better."

Hiram walked up a few steps away from Martin and held out the knife, handle first. "I should have properly introduced myself. Hiram Salvadore aka the Rhinoplasty Killer."

Martin frowned. "Rhinoplasty?" he asked.

"Yes, I'm, or at least was, a serial killer like you. Only instead of hands, sorry, *right* hands, I collect noses. There's just something about the symmetry of a perfect nose that I can't resist."

In the beginning, a much younger Doctor Hiram Salvadore stood in an operating room dressed in scrubs. A full medical staff surrounded the operating table. On the table, a woman laid with a breathing tube in her mouth. Pen marks denoting planned surgical incisions peppered her nose, which was bathed in a burnt orange colored disinfectant. A protective set of goggles sat firmly on her closed eyelids. Next to her head, an anesthesiologist monitored her vital signs. He looked at Hiram and smiled.

"She's completely out. Ready when you are Doctor Salvadore," the middle-aged man said.

Hiram sweated profusely, and he hadn't started operating yet. He looked down at the patient and something inside him broke. He'd performed dozens of nose jobs this first two years in private practice, but this case had been too much. The nurse mopped his brow.

"Are you all right, Doctor?" the nurse asked.

"Why does she want to change it? This nose is perfect as it is," Hiram said in a kind of trance.

"I'm sorry, what?" the nurse asked.

Hiram stepped back from the operating table, shaking his head.

"I can't do it," Hiram whispered. "I can't do it anymore." He pulled off his surgical mask and removed his gloves. He slammed the blue gloves down on the instrument table, jarring the surgical instruments from their careful arrangement.

"Wake her up," Hiram said as he pulled off his surgical gown. "No surgery today."

Hiram walked out of the operating room, abandoning rhinoplasty in his practice forever.

Hiram shrugged his shoulders at Martin. "A compulsion really, but then I suppose you know what I'm talking about. That's why they call you the Handyman Killer—always cutting off the right hand."

"It's the forearm and hand, actually... from the elbow," Martin replied in a daze. He turned, walked back to the freezer door, and opened it. The arms continued their frenetic activity, attempting to loosen themselves from the meat hooks they dangled from. Hiram followed and stopped just a few steps behind.

"Yeah, I meant to ask about that. Why don't they call you the Army Man or something like that?"

Martin looked at Hiram and just shook his head slowly.

"You know, I carved the noses off while they were still

alive," Hiram said in an analytic tone, as if giving a speech at a medical symposium. "Sometimes they were unconscious, but they were always alive until I finished."

Hiram frowned and cocked his head. "You know, it seems kind of sick now that I don't have the passion for it anymore," Hiram added. "Perhaps a little cruel. Some of them definitely deserved it, though."

Martin closed his eyes for a moment. He breathed the cool air into his lungs deeply and grit his teeth. "I got regular beatings from my dad and then both stepfathers. They always led with the right," Martin said. He opened his eyes and touched the closest forearm to him, as if petting a dog or cat in his care. "Remove the right hand. Remove the threat." Martin frowned and walked back out of the freezer.

"Well, I never got beaten up by a nose," Hiram said with a sniff. "Perhaps we are different. Anyway, I just came to watch, not really advise so much."

Martin looked down at his chest, covered in grimy fluids that had squirted from Hiram's heart when he grabbed it. He pulled his shirt off and put it in the garbage. "Watch?" Martin asked as he walked over to the sink. He washed his chest off as Hector leered at him from the jar. Martin frowned at Hector.

"Perhaps I didn't make myself clear. Well, you were busy killing me, so I suppose you weren't paying that much attention." Hiram paced lazily back and forth while Martin cleaned himself off. "I performed a rather complex ritual, combining several religions and ethnic rituals, mostly Santeria, Haitian and gypsy, meant to force all our victims to come after us and kill us. Then you killed me, whereupon all my victims will now come after you as well, since I'm obviously already dead. You've got quite the army on your trail."

"How do I beat them?" Martin asked as he toweled off.

"Haven't the foggiest. My only desire is the final one I had—to see them rip the flesh from your bones. I'm still very keen for that."

"I don't intend to let that happen," Martin replied as he went back to the front office and opened a wardrobe filled with cleaned, pressed clothing, including underwear, socks, and boxes of shoes. He looked down at his pants and shoes and shook his head. He stripped down to his underwear, pulled his wallet from the soiled pants and got changed into all new clothing.

"Oh, good luck. As I'm sure you've noticed, the dead have stopped resting. Even little pieces of them are still trying to get to you and kill you."

"I can hold off a lot of attackers in this place," Martin said, as he waved his hands around at the warehouse. Hiram looked around and nodded. Martin quickly folded more clothes and placed them carefully in a small suitcase. He put four more pairs of shoes in a separate duffel bag. He walked his soiled clothing and shoes and dropped them in the garbage can with his shirt.

"Oh, it's a nice fortress, except for that front door. A hundred undead pressing against it are going to splinter that thing pretty quickly." Hiram grinned. "I recommend staying put. *Magnifico!*"

Martin looked at the sturdy wooden door, but realized a simple battering ram would have it down in seconds. The unyielding press of a hundred or more undead trying to get at him probably would have the same effect.

"Uh, maybe the police..." Martin wondered as Hiram finished that brief contemplation fairly quickly.

"Oh, that's a fine idea, too," Hiram said as he chuckled. "Ahem, 'Excuse me, officer, I'm the Handyman killer. Could you please protect me from all my undead victims?' The undead will tear you apart in your padded cell. In case you were wondering, I'm also okay with that plan."

"Well, what do you suggest, old man?"

"Lie down and let them rip the flesh from your bones. It's going to happen eventually, and I'd really like to see it."

"Over my dead body," Martin snorted.

"That's the spirit!" Hiram exclaimed.

Martin stopped and looked at Hiram. He examined him from head to toe for a moment. Aside from a strange predilection to wear a suit coat but no shirt, he seemed a perfectly normal, albeit dead, elderly man.

"How did you get here so fast?" Martin asked.

"I drove," Hiram replied.

"Great," Martin said. He walked over to Hector and picked up the jar he was in. "Zombies that can drive is not a plus for me."

Martin dumped the water and Hector's head out into the sink.

"About time!" Hector shouted. "That was like drowning in piss!"

"I had no idea they'd be so articulate," Hiram said as he walked near the sink to watch Hector moving his jaw and wiggling his ears. He snorted and squirted water from his nose.

"Yeah, lucky me," Martin said. "He's a fresh kill."

"Beheading isn't your normal *modus operandi*,"

Hiram said.

"Let's just say it's a bad idea to mug a serial killer," Martin replied as he rinsed the jar out and washed it.

"I can see where that could be a bad life choice," Hiram responded as he frowned at Hector.

"Guess drowning me didn't shut me up, eh?" Hector piped in as his head rolled around in the soapy water. He spit out some of the water as it dripped from the jar. "How about stuffing my mouth with your jugular vein? I promise I won't bite! Cross my heart and hope to die."

Hiram grunted.

"Did your little spell include sarcasm, by chance?" Martin asked as he set the jar back on the counter.

"Must've been the Romani in it."

Martin put on a fresh pair of gloves, went back into the front office, and looked through the supplies there for a burlap sack. He took it to the freezer.

As Martin opened the freezer door, the severed limbs increased their frenzied gyrations once again. Martin selected the arm closest to the door and worked it off the hook. It wriggled around like a live fish. The hand kept grabbing for him as he stuffed the arm into the sack. After wrangling it inside, he tied the top of the sack, carried it out and set it next to the sink.

He picked Hector's skull up by the hair again and put it back in the jar. "Hey, hey!" Hector exclaimed. "I can tell Mom I joined the Marines! I'm a jarhead!"

Martin grabbed a lid and screwed it on top. He took the jar and sack to the front door, set them down as he unlocked the door, checked outside, and noticed Hiram's white sedan sitting out front. Sighing wistfully, he picked everything up.

Inside the jar, Hector began singing 'From the Halls of Montezuma' as Martin jostled his head while walking to the car. Martin found a small amount of comfort that the jar muted the disembodied singer.

Martin opened the trunk, put all the items inside, including Hector, and arranged them neatly in the sections laid out in the trunk. Returning to the warehouse, he removed the surgical gloves and threw them into the garbage before removing the garbage bag and walking it back to the furnace. Disposing of it all inside the furnace, he closed the door with a loud clank. He left it all burning to ash as he secured the walk-in freezer again. One last time, he washed his hands and cleaned the sink again.

"Tidy," Hiram said with a smirk. Martin glared at him as he walked by and opened a storage cabinet near the front office. He grabbed several weapons and walked back past Hiram, who watched with bemusement.

"Never can be too prepared," Martin said with a grin. He grabbed his suitcase, duffel bag and the weapons and took them outside to the car, placing everything inside the sectioned areas. As he closed the trunk, he heard Hector's muffled voice shout, "Wait! I'm afraid of the dark! Hold me!"

Martin went back inside. After a brief visit to the furnace to ensure everything had been thoroughly destroyed, he shut the furnace down. If he wound up living through this, he'd return to clean the molten metal from the furnace floor. He snagged the bat with one hand and grabbed Hiram with the other as he walked back out the warehouse front door.

"We're going on a little road trip. I like to keep my enemies where I can see them," Martin said as he stopped to lock the door.

"Fine by me," Hiram replied. "I like to keep you where I can see the flesh stripped—"

"Yeah, I got it," Martin interrupted and grabbed Hiram's arm again. "Let's go."

Martin directed Hiram to sit in the back seat as he took the front and set the bat down on the seat next to him. As they drove away from the warehouse, Martin pulled out his cell phone and made a call.

In her darkened bedroom, Bibi Riley woke to the phone ringing by her bed. She turned on the light and looked at the clock. It was a little after one o'clock in the morning. She grabbed the phone with her left hand and cradled it with her neck. She pulled her long, dirty blonde hair out from between her head and the phone. "Hello?"

"Hey, Bibi," Martin's voice replied.

Bibi's face lit up. "Hey baby! I didn't expect to hear from you tonight."

In Martin's car, he scanned the surrounding road for any signs of police activity. He sighed. "Hey, sorry to be calling so late. I need to drop by and talk about something urgent."

"It's after one, baby," Bibi replied coyly. "I mean, I have to work tomorrow. Being up all night... well..."

"I know," Martin said as he nodded reflexively. "It can't wait. I gotta see you before I leave town."

Bibi bolted upright in bed. She was suddenly wide awake. The right arm sleeve of her baggy black nightgown hung empty at her side empty. She gripped the phone in her left hand. "Leave town? Why? What's the matter?"

"I'll tell you when I get there. Not on the phone," Martin replied cryptically.

"Umm, okay, baby," Bibi replied and then bit her lip. She hung up the phone and jumped out of bed. She paced the room.

"Lights full," she said to the automated system in the house. The room lit up, revealing framed, heavy metal posters and biker paraphernalia on the walls.

"Fuck that," Bibi said and strode to her closet. She pulled it open and grabbed a suitcase. She threw it on the bed and expertly opened it with her left hand. In quick, efficient movements, she whirled around the bedroom, grabbing clothes and packing the suitcase with only her left hand.

In the car, Martin sighed as he tucked the phone back in his jacket pocket.

"One more killing before you go?" Hiram asked with a chuckle.

"No, I just need to tell her goodbye," Martin replied calmly.

"Touching. Nothing says I love you like confessing that you're a serial killer."

"Yeah," Martin replied as he squinted in the rearview mirror at the chatty dead man. "I thought you'd approve. More importantly, I need you to verify my story."

"Nothing verifies a horror story like a serial killer zombie," Hiram said and looked out the window. "The ending of the story will be something to die for."

As they passed a side street, several zombies walked toward the road Martin drove on. When he passed, they crossed the street, moving toward the car racing away down the road.

CHAPTER 7

ibi walked by the TV wearing a long-sleeved bathrobe with the right arm tucked up. She carried an empty plastic bag into the kitchen as the television special report blared on. "Earlier this evening, two known gang members were reportedly killed during an apparent mugging attempt at a car wash, although no bodies were recovered. Police are on the lookout for a magenta sedan that was seen in the area," the newscaster reported.

Bibi replaced the bag in the empty kitchen trash can and then moved into the bathroom.

"There are also some strange reports of the dead walking, but nothing has been confirmed. Police are saying the zombie reports are nothing more than a prank for Halloween, just a bunch of kids wandering around trying to scare folks."

In the bathroom, Bibi put on makeup and worked on her hair. The voices of the news report faded as she thought back to when she first met Martin.

One of her only friends outside of the biker bar she used to call her home away from home had invited her out for a night at the new ax throwing place. She attended, but felt the mechanics of throwing an axe didn't suit her prosthetic arm. Her one armed attempts hadn't produced stellar results, but she managed to make it to the target a quarter of the time.

Martin attended with a group of his sales team from the dealership. She didn't remember exactly when he first noticed her, but before the night was out, they'd broken off from the others and conversed at a table by themselves.

"Look," Bibi said as she patted his hand, "I don't want this to get awkward, but before we go much further, I want to be candid. I don't want any surprises scaring you off later. I'd rather they scared you off right now."

"Tell me," Martin said with a smooth intensity that made her pause for a moment. His eyes looked into hers, and she felt her heart flutter for a moment. A tear threatened to form as she figured this would be the last moment she'd feel like that with this handsome Hispanic man who'd taken a liking to her. She raised her prosthetic arm and shrugged.

"It's not real," she said.

Martin glanced at her arm and grinned. "Is it an illusion? Are you a magician too?" he replied.

"No," Bibi replied. "I lost it in an accident."

"Well, it appears you have found it again, so no harm, no foul," Martin said. He cocked his eyebrow, and she narrowed her eyes at him.

"It's prosthetic," she said plainly.

"Oh, so it is real!" Martin replied with a laugh. "You had me worried there for a second."

"I'm missing this arm," Bibi said and gave him a wry grin.

"You are missing nothing," Martin said. "You are perfect in every way."

"But—" Bibi protested. Martin put his finger to her lips.

"Everything you are now is perfect. It's enough. There's nothing in my eyes that's missing. Everyone has something going on. When it's a portion of their personality missing, trust me—that's a lot harder to love."

Bibi dropped her hand and set it on his. "So you don't mind," she said.

"It never even crossed my mind," Martin replied as he caressed her cheek. "You have nothing to apologize for—you are perfect in my eyes and always will be and, hopefully..." he paused and winked at her. "That means I might get to go on a proper first date, say, next Friday?"

Bibi smiled at him. "That would be nice."

Bibi looked at her face in the mirror and applied some lip gloss. She finished and smiled at her reflection. "It was very nice," she told herself. She packed up the makeup and walked back into the bedroom, and placed the makeup bag in her suitcase.

Martin pulled up in front of Bibi's small suburban condo and turned off the car. He sat in the car as he tapped his fingers on the steering wheel and glanced at her condo more than once.

"We're just going to sit here and wait for them to come kill you? How pleasant," Hiram said in the back seat.

"I've never broken up with anyone before. They usually break up with me," Martin said. "I can't imagine it will go well. Maybe I'll be fortunate and she'll kill me before your zombies do."

"That won't do," Hiram said, wrinkling his nose. "I went to a lot of trouble for the undead to hunt you down like the miserable dog you are. Don't disappoint me."

"Oh, yeah, we wouldn't want that." Martin scoffed.

He opened the door and got out. Hiram exited the car as well.

Bibi heard the car doors shut and ran to look out the window. She spotted Martin walking toward the house with someone else and frowned. "The fucker's leaving town with someone else?" she muttered as she walked to the front door. "Over my dead body!"

She opened the front door and hugged Martin with her left arm and the stub of her right. He kissed her reluctantly, and she pulled him inside, with Hiram close behind.

"Hi honey! Who's your friend?" she asked as she looked Hiram up and down. She wrinkled her nose and cocked her head at him.

"Oh," Martin said as he looked behind him. "This is Hiram—he's more of an acquaintance than a friend."

"What happened to your arm?" Hiram asked.

"Nice manners, Hiram. I lost it in a motorcycle accident. Turns out helmets don't protect arms so much."

Hiram closed the door and sighed. "Ah," Hiram replied and shook his head. "Knowing your boyfriend, I thought it would be a more interesting and sickening story. Now, it just... fits."

Bibi frowned at Hiram, and Martin brought her attention back to him with a gentle touch on the cheek. She looked at her beloved and leaned into his caress.

"Sweetheart, I'm going to have to go away for a while," Martin said.

"Oh, I don't like it when you have to go away," Bibi replied with a pout. "How long this time?"

"Maybe forever."

"You're breaking up with me? What the fuck? Are you

gay?" Bibi yelled. She pointed at Hiram. "Did you bring your new metalhead cosplay lover along? Is that what this is?"

"Metal head?" Hiram asked with a chuckle. He looked down at his clothes and realized it was all dark clothing. He thought he looked more goth than anything else.

"No, I'm not gay," Martin said with a sigh. "I'm a serial killer."

Bibi stepped back for a moment. She looked at Hiram and then back at Martin. "So, why are you leaving again?" she asked as she put her lone arm across her chest like she was folding her arms.

Hiram frowned at her and then squinted at her face. "You have a lovely nose," Hiram remarked. Martin punched Hiram in the chest hard, knocking the undead man to the floor.

"You leave her the fuck alone!" Martin shouted.

"Are you going to kill him?" Bibi asked in hushed anticipation.

"Already did. He's a zombie," Martin replied.

"Really?" Bibi replied with a sneer. "Prove it."

Hiram sighed as he got to his feet. He opened his coat, revealing his bare chest with now clear cut marks around one side of his chest around the heart. Hiram pushed his fingers into the knife wound Martin had made in him twice and pulled open his chest. Hiram's ghastly beating heart pumped slowly, squirting a bit of fluid out onto the floor of Bibi's entryway.

Bibi gasped and covered her mouth. She ran to the kitchen sink and puked into it. Hiram shrugged and pushed his chest back into place.

"Looks like she can't handle the serial killer lifestyle," Hiram said.

"She's not a killer. She's just dating one," Martin said to Hiram and then turned to Bibi. "Sweetheart, we really need to go. Aside from Prince Charming here, all the other zombies really want to kill me. I don't want you to get hurt when they get to me."

"Other zombies?" Bibi asked. She took one look at Hiram and gagged again. She bent over and threw up again in the sink.

"Genius here created a bunch of zombies out of our victims to hunt us down. So there's a shitload of undead out for our heads. I just felt like I owed you a goodbye."

"Fuck that. I'm coming with you. My life sucked before you came along. Give me two minutes," Bibi said as she wiped her mouth with a towel and left the room.

As she finished packing her toiletries, Bibi's thoughts returned to her last visit to the Lazy Ass Bar. As she played pool with her sometime pal, Deanna, a brunette biker chick with large breasts and a crazy amount of cleavage showing in her tight top, the ever present drunks approached with a sneer. Deanna watched from the bar stool she sat on, nursing her drink.

Frank, a big dude with hair everywhere except a spreading bald spot on his head, patted Bibi on her shoulder. "Hey baby, show these guys your stump," Frank slurred as he nearly stumbled onto the pool table. Bibi slid her pool cue into her artificial right hand and set in on the floor. She put her left hand on her hip and shook her head at Frank.

"Frank, you're drunk. Go home before you do something stupid," she replied. "Or stupider, anyway."

"Hey, sweetheart, I was just telling these guys how hot you get when someone strokes your stump," Frank shouted, spitting with each syllable. The gathering throng of bar patrons hooted and hollered in appreciation of Frank's statement.

"Maybe you can should them how stupid I was to date such a pathetic creep," Bibi replied with a sneer.

Deanna snickered and took a swig of her beer. She folded her arms to watch the show.

"Awww, don't be like that, Stumpy!" Frank hollered and laughed along with everyone else in the bar, including Deanna.

"*That's it!*" Bibi screamed and put a roundhouse kick into Frank's chest, knocking him across the bar. He struggled to get up from the collapsed furniture around him, half from being stunned and half from being piss drunk. The other drunk bikers looked in shock at Frank and then shouted angrily at Bibi as they advanced on her. Bibi picked her cue stick back up off the floor and busted it in half on the pool table. She waved the jagged end at the drunk crowd.

"Looks like I need to stake some vampires tonight," she shouted at the throng.

The drunks grumbled as they realized they really weren't in any shape to mess with her and backed off. Deanna slammed her own pool stick on the table.

"Dammit, Bibi!" Deanna shouted. "Why are you being such a bitch?"

"You too, Deanna? Fuck all of you then!" Bibi screamed. She picked up her beer and drained it before slamming the empty mug down on the pool table. She walked out of the bar, slamming the door shut behind her.

Now Bibi stared at the suitcase. "Assholes," she muttered. She double checked her suitcase and crammed a few more necessities in it. After dropping her robe, she hastily put on her prosthetic arm and got dressed in shorts, a long-sleeved pink shirt and cowboy boots. Retrieving a machete and sheath from her closet, she held them in her hands for a moment.

Martin had gifted her with the machete after their second date. She'd commented that guns were unwieldy and, as he had seen the first night they met, throwing an axe wasn't a great fit either.

"This weapon," Martin assured her. "Only requires one hand. That is, in fact, the way it is most often used. You'll be hacking, slicing and chopping your way through the underbrush of life in no time."

She stood in her bedroom, holding the handle in her hand, and smiled. Sniffing back the tears that threatened to burst forth, she strapped on the sheath, machete lying flat against her back and walked back into the living room with her suitcase.

"Everyone treated me like a leper once I lost my arm. You're the only one who loved me for what I was," Bibi said as Martin looked up at her.

"Or for what you didn't have," Hiram said as he stepped up next to Martin.

In a swift blur of motion, Bibi pulled her machete out and swung it between Hiram's legs, stopping just before connecting.

"I'll cut your prick off and shove it down your undead throat if you piss me off!" Bibi screamed in Hiram's face.

"Not that I could feel it, but I'm sufficiently horrified by that act that I'll leave you and your precious nose alone," Hiram sniffed. "Besides, I noticed it's flawed, anyway.

Wouldn't look good in my collection."

"Good. If you hurt Martin, I'll feed you your undead ass too."

"I think we understand each other," Hiram said with a chuckle. "I don't want to take part in harming him. I just want to watch. I'm a death voyeur—just along for the show."

Bibi turned to Martin and cocked her head. "Why are we bringing him along? He smells like shit."

"I need him to prove the zombie problem to the authorities," Martin replied. He looked at Hiram and sighed.

"We're going to the police?" Bibi asked.

Martin shook his head. "Wrong authorities," he said. "We need a little more firepower to fight off what's coming."

"We're going to ask the gangs for help?"

Martin laughed. "No, we need industrial firepower. We're going to Area 51."

"Oh, nice," Bibi replied as she wrinkled her nose. "We have to drive all that way with dead boy in the car? We better stop for a shitload of air fresheners."

"Nice boots, by the way," Hiram chimed in.

"They're called shit kickers, asshole. Try not to be on the receiving end of them," Bibi replied with a smile. She put her machete back and picked up her suitcase. She walked out of the house.

Martin and Hiram followed. Martin locked the door behind them. Hiram hung back with Martin as he watched Bibi walk ahead. Bibi put her suitcase in the back seat. She climbed into the front passenger seat.

"Charming girl," Hiram muttered. "I can see the attraction."

"She is threatening to everyone but me and she can

wield a machete like she was born in the jungle. What's not to love?" Martin replied and looked at Hiram with a grin. Martin walked around the car as Hiram got in the back seat, pushing Bibi's suitcase across behind the driver's side. Martin got in and reached to start the car.

A zombie hand reached in from outside the car and grabbed at Martin. Bibi jumped out of the car and hacked away at the zombie, separating the arm attacking Martin, who threw the arm as far as he could while Bibi cut the legs off the squirming zombie. It fell to the ground and groaned as it tried to crawl toward the car, virtually ignoring the woman who had just diced it into pieces.

"Get in the car!" Martin shouted. Bibi glanced up from the hacked up zombie and saw a dozen more shambling shapes in the dark coming toward them. As the undead passed through the halo of the streetlights, Bibi could see they were all in various states of decomposition, some whole bodies, others just legs walking or other decaying partial body parts moving toward them.

"Oh shit!" Bibi groaned. She ran back to the car and climbed in.

"How many of these fuckers are there?" Bibi asked.

Martin started up the car and pulled away from the curb, squealing the tires.

"Well," Hiram replied from the back seat calmly. "Best I can reckon, somewhere around five hundred."

Martin drove through a zombie, which tumbled over the top of the car. "What? How many did you kill?" Martin asked as he swerved around most of the zombies littering the road in front of him.

"About four hundred," Hiram replied as he looked up,

lost in thought. "Harder to keep track when you get older. So I just average it out to about one a week."

"Huh," Martin replied. "Me too."

"You guys have been busy!" Bibi shouted as she struggled to put on her seatbelt.

The sedan knocked two zombies down and ran over them. As the car jumped wildly over bodies, the car dovetailed. Martin fought to maintain control.

"Well, I'm older than you. Probably been at it longer," Hiram said and folded his hands across his lap.

"I've only really been going for five years. About the same rate, but I started a little slow. More like two hundred."

Hiram frowned. "That's more than you admitted in the building."

"I was being conservative, and I only counted the right arm kills, not the school."

"Well," Hiram said. "At this rate, you're not really eliminating any of the six hundred then, just slowing them down."

Martin hit another particularly bloated zombie, and it exploded on impact. Martin turned on the windshield wipers and squirted fluid on the windshield.

"Well," Hiram said with a laugh. "I don't think that one is going to be a problem."

"Dammit, I just washed this car!" Martin screamed. Hiram giggled in the back seat. Martin looked ahead and saw dozens of zombies; looking in the rearview mirror, he saw the same thing. "Wish I had a tank. Hold on."

Martin stepped on the gas and the car darted forward. As he barreled down the street, he tried to avoid as many of the zombies as possible. Because they were so numerous, some zombies got their limbs into the car. The arms, hands and fingers that got inside were quickly severed by the window frames.

As they turned a corner, a zombie skull embedded itself in the passenger side headlight like a ghoulish hood ornament. As he raced down the new street, Martin looked down to see a mass of squirming zombie limbs littering the inside of the car. Martin stopped the car and jumped out.

"Get them out of the car!" he shouted. Bibi grabbed squirming body parts and flung them out the window. Hiram picked up a scrambling hand and forearm, which he examined for a moment, fascinated. He shrugged his shoulders and set the arm on the roof of the car.

"Go!" Bibi shouted as Martin got back in the car and gunned the engine. Smoke billowed from the screeching tires as he took off down the road. The arm on the roof of the car tumbled down, but grabbed the edge of the rear bumper and hung on. The trio drove off into the night.

All over Southern California, zombies walked across streets and changed their trajectory to follow the fleeing vehicle. They continued their mindless, undead trek across parks, gardens, and backyards.

Outside Margaret Baretta's home in Fullerton, a male zombie stumbled through a large garden, uprooting a beautiful collection of flowers. Margaret watched from inside the house. She shouted in anger and ran out the front door of the house. She ran toward the shambling figure, armed with an umbrella and an attitude.

"You damn hooligans! Always tearing up my flowers!" she shouted as she hit the zombie with her umbrella. The zombie paid her no attention and continued stumbling forward.

"Get your drunk ass out of my garden!" she shouted. She swung with all her might, both hands on the umbrella, and hit the zombie on the right side. It knocked his arm off. The wiggling limb fell to the ground with a thud. Margaret stopped swinging the umbrella and backed up.

"Oh my word!" she muttered.

The zombie looked at her and she finally noticed the decaying face. Flesh hung off the skull, and the eyeballs were dried out, giant yellow prunes rolling around in the eye sockets. Margaret screamed in horror.

The zombie made a gurgling sound at her and reached down to retrieve its arm. Margaret ran back into her house screaming. The zombie pushed its arm back into place. It fell off again and crawled forward on its own. The zombie shook its head and walked away into the night.

CHAPTER 8

Bibi snuggled under a blanket in the front seat as the cool night air blew in through the windows. Martin stared ahead while he sipped coffee from a plain white cup. The lights of the city faded behind them as they came down the mountain. A dark blanket of nothing enveloped the desert landscape ahead of them, broken only by the shine of the full moon above.

"I never realized how boring being a zombie could be," Hiram said, breaking the silence. "Not a lot of excitement."

"Did you expect something else?" Martin replied, glancing in the rear-view mirror. Hiram was shrouded by the dark of the night, but Martin was also checking for any pursuing police vehicles.

"I didn't actually expect to be a zombie. Thought I would stay dead. Although, it could be worse; I could be in your shoes," Hiram replied.

"Why is that worse?" Martin asked. He sipped his coffee again and looked out over the vast night sky, searching for helicopters or small planes–anything that could be a sign of pursuit.

"Well, you're a complete failure as a serial killer. None of your victims are staying dead."

Martin laughed. "Neither are yours. And you're a zombie."

"*Touché*," Hiram replied.

Martin stared ahead in the distance and felt an odd pang of loss. He looked over at Bibi and his spirits rose a bit, but they didn't replace that hole he felt in his soul now.

"Ya know, death used to be the ultimate comfort to me," Martin said. "I win, the other person loses. Now I can't trust death."

"That's a very philosophical position for such a bloodthirsty killer."

"I took a lot of philosophy classes in college," Martin replied as he checked the rearview mirror for any approaching vehicles. "In between kills."

"At least you were trying to better yourself," Hiram said with a grunt. "I simply embraced the killing. I perfected my technique, had elaborate exit strategies and planned out my dumping grounds with an abundance of caution. That's why I have more kills than you."

"Yeah, not exactly something to be proud of."

"I never expected the joy to go out of it," Hiram said as he looked out the window at the impenetrable darkness. The slightly darker ribbon of road stretched out ahead of them to the horizon. "I made it a weekly event, like grocery shopping."

"Brings a whole new meaning to 'Clean-up on aisle two.'" They laughed. Bibi stirred but stayed asleep.

"I never really planned mine out like you," Martin replied. He took a swig of the cooling coffee. "I was more impulsive. Sure, I was careful, but most of my victims weren't planned out well ahead of time."

"Mmm, kind of a shame. Cut down before you even hit your stride. Not that I would've done anything different. Still keen to see you pulled apart."

"I ain't dead yet," Martin said. He finished the coffee and set the cup inside the plastic bag from the mini-mart that sat on the seat between him and Bibi.

"I give you a week, tops."

"Hopeful on your part. Maybe you'll die again of boredom first."

"Not this week," Hiram said and chuckled.

Officer Carlyle stood by his police cruiser and stared at the two walking figures coming toward him slowly. The orange hued street lights gave them the appearance of fiery demons from hell stalking their earthly prey in an unyielding march. He shook his head to get the image out of his mind, raised the transmitter to his mouth, and held the button.

"This is Officer Carlyle on Wilkins Ave. I've got them in sight. They're not doing anything but walking. Over."

"Officer Carlyle, we have a civilian down at the morgue. Suspects may be hostile. Use extreme caution. Over."

"Ten-four," Officer Carlyle replied, as he set the transmitter back in the holder. Swallowing hard, he stood up, pulled out his flashlight and walked forward with one hand on his holster, ready to pull his weapon. When he illuminated the two subjects with a beam of light, he stopped walking forward, even though they never stopped moving.

The desiccated remains he saw in front of him could

be described as nothing more than skeletons with hunks of flesh hanging haphazardly dressed in clothing that only hung on because it was melded to the bits of flesh. He took out his gun and pointed it at the two suspects.

"Halt! This is the police. You are under arrest for assault. Lie face down on the ground with your hands behind your back."

The zombies continued walking toward him.

"Stop or I will have to use deadly force!" he shouted as he took a step back. The figures appeared to not hear him and continued as before. He fired his weapon into one zombie and then the other. The bullets appeared to pass right through the clothing and out the other side hitting nothing else. Unabated, the zombies continued walking toward him.

"What the hell?" Officer Carlyle muttered. He reached to his other side and pulled out his high-voltage stun gun and fired at the first zombie. The sparks from the electricity lit up the clothing like kindling and the zombie was on fire within a few seconds. It continued walking forward. Officer Carlyle retreated to the other side of his car. The zombies continued walking forward, passing by him on the other side of his car. The one that was still on fire seemed completely unfazed by its predicament. The policeman reached in from the passenger side and grabbed his radio.

"Cannot stop suspects. Deadly force had no effect. Well, one of them is on fire, but hasn't stopped walking," he said into the radio, his voice shaking with adrenaline and fear.

"I'm sorry, Officer Carlyle, could you repeat that?" came the crackling response from the dispatcher.

"I cannot stop suspects. Request SWAT team," he replied. He continued holding the button as he watched the flaming zombie clear the end of his car and continue walking down the street. "And a fire truck."

In the dispatch office, the dispatcher had a look of confusion on her face. She waved at her supervisor, who walked over immediately. The supervisor looked a bit harried.

"Gina, this officer just fired shots and a taser at the suspects and they didn't stop. They're just walking," the dispatcher said and shrugged her shoulders.

Gina looked over at the other dispatchers, working the phones with frowns and shaking their heads. There were echoes of "What" and "Can you repeat that" coming from most of them.

"I think we need to call the chief," Gina said and ran from the room.

Pavel Andreovich walked into the security office at the Valentine Mall. He whistled a merry tune as the night was just as uneventful as the hundred before it. As he stepped through the door, Anton, Pavel's brother, looked at him with a face gone white. The two brothers had both immigrated to the United States just a year before and had been fortunate to find work together on the night shift at the mall.

"You look troubled," Pavel said. "Do we have an intruder?"

Anton scooted his rolling chair backward and pointed at the security monitors. The doors of the main entrance had just buckled. Half a dozen figures pushed through the debris and stumbled forward, walking with purpose into the mall. As Pavel looked, one of the monitors assigned to a zoom camera pinpointed one figure entering the mall. As the camera zoomed in, Pavel saw a skeletal hand dangling from the left of the figure and, even more notably, the figure in tattered rags had no head.

"Shouldn't we stop them?" Anton asked in a shaky voice.

"I'm not going down there," Pavel said, shaking his head. "Call the 911 number. Let the police handle this." Pavel locked the door to the security office.

Anton picked up the phone on the desk and started dialing.

Martin parked his car in the motel lot away from the office so as not to raise any suspicions about the state of his car and the passengers within. When he stopped the car, Bibi woke up and blinked her eyes rapidly as she looked at Martin. She smiled groggily, and then her eyes went wide. She bolted upright and looked in the back seat. Hiram cocked his head and waved at her.

"Ugh," she said, wrinkling her nose. "It wasn't just a nightmare."

"Good morning to you too," Hiram replied.

"Still night, asshole. Try to keep up," Bibi said. She looked at Martin. "What are we doing?"

"It's been a long ass day. We all need some rest," Martin said, and then glanced at Hiram. "Well, most of us need sleep."

"I could drive," Bibi suggested.

"Not without some good rest. I'm going to wake up the night manager and get a room for a few hours. Be nice to get a shower too," Martin said as he opened the door. Bibi looked back at Hiram.

"Not all of us, asshole. You'll be just as stinky," she

said and got out of the car.

Hiram shrugged his shoulders.

As the car doors slammed shut, the disembodied arm hanging from the rear bumper dropped to the ground. It started crawling away from the car. Bibi grabbed her suitcase from behind the driver's seat and pulled it out onto the small sidewalk running the length of the motel. It was pitch black outside, so she didn't notice the zombie arm pulled along by its hand headed for the office.

Martin entered the small office for the motel and rang the bell on the counter. No one responded. He looked around briefly and then banged on the bell a few more times. Finally, a bedraggled hotel clerk emerged from a back room and squinted at Martin.

"What the hell, dude? It's the middle of the night!" the clerk said.

"My girlfriend and I need a room. Preferably number sixteen over there by my car," Martin said as he pointed to the lone vehicle in the parking lot.

"Sure thing. You got the pick of rooms since they're all vacant," the clerk replied as he rubbed his face and sat down in the chair. "That'll be $78 with tax. Checkout is by noon sharp. Credit card?"

The clerk held his palm out.

"How about we just do cash?" Martin said.

"Sure thing. We require a $100 deposit on the room refundable when you check out."

Martin reached into his back pocket and pulled out his wallet. He handed the clerk four one hundred-dollar bills. "Put us down for two nights, just in case we don't get out by noon. And keep the change," Martin said.

The clerk took the bills and used a highlighter marker on them to make sure they weren't counterfeit. He raised his eyebrows and grabbed a key for room sixteen.

"Here ya go," the clerk said and handed Martin two bottles of water from behind the counter and the key. "Complimentary water bottles. I'm afraid we have nothing else to offer. There's a vending machine by the ice machine, but it just has chips in it. Only thing that won't melt in the heat."

"Thank you. Sorry for waking you," Martin said.

"Not a problem," the clerk replied, waving the four hundred dollars. "You certainly made it worth my while."

Martin left the office and stepped off the sidewalk onto the asphalt parking lot, just missing the zombie arm pulling itself up the edge of the sidewalk, barely illuminated by the lights in the office. The arm popped up into the air, grasping at Martin's pant leg, but didn't connect with anything but air. Martin walked over to Bibi and gave her an embrace and a kiss.

"Got a room for two nights if needed. We can just rest and recuperate," Martin said.

"Great idea," Hiram piped in from the back seat of the car. "My dumping grounds were largely in this desert. We should have the place surrounded within a day."

"You're staying out here—the dead don't need a bed," Martin sneered.

"Undead," Hiram replied.

"Whatever," Martin said.

"Asshole any way you slice it," Bibi said.

Martin retrieved a fresh set of clothes from the trunk.

"Hey *vato!*" Hector said in a muted voice from within

his jar.

"Hey nightmare," Martin responded and then shut the trunk.

They disappeared into the motel room, and Hiram sighed. He noticed movement on the ground coming toward the car. He could just barely make out the zombie arm heading toward the motel room. Hiram laughed.

The zombie arm crawled along the wall and found the air conditioner just off the ground. The fingers felt their way around the metal box, but couldn't find a way inside the room. Climbing on top of the air conditioner, it caught the edge of the window, and pulled its way along the edge of the window. As it started going up the frame, it felt for an opening but the closed window offered none.

Bibi tossed her suitcase onto the bed next to the clean clothes Martin had just laid down. She turned and embraced Martin. They kissed, and Martin relaxed for a moment. Engulfed in her warm embrace was the only place he felt normal. Reluctantly, he pushed her back a few inches.

"I need a shower," Martin whispered. "I have the fluids of more than one dead person on these clothes and my skin."

"So romantic," Bibi said with a smirk. "Is it okay if I freshen up while you're showering?"

"Absolutely," Martin replied. He got a big grin on his face and peeled off his clothing. As he removed each piece, he tossed it into the corner of the room furthest away from everything.

Bibi looked at the pile of clothes and then back at Martin curiously. "You're not going to launder them in the sink?" Bibi asked.

"I've brought along enough extras. I can just burn these in a pit if we have the chance before we leave. I'm sure as hell not going to try to clean them," Martin replied with a laugh.

"I'll put them in a garbage bag, seal them up and get them out of here," Bibi said as she pulled the liner from the small trash can sitting near the door. Martin caught her arm before she could reach for the discarded clothes. He touched her face gently and gave her a soft kiss.

"You're the best," Martin said. He let her go and retreated to the bathroom.

Bibi touched her cheek for a moment where he'd touched her and smiled. She slipped out of her own clothes and quickly tossed them, along with Martin's discarded clothes, into the bag. She opened the door and set the bag outside the door. As she turned around to go back in, the zombie arm made a swipe at her back but missed and fell to the ground. Bibi didn't notice the undead activity and went back into the room, closing the door behind her.

"Well," Hiram said with a sigh. "You get an A for effort, random, disembodied zombie arm."

Inside the motel room, Bibi removed her prosthetic arm, set it on the nightstand next to the bed, and quickly joined Martin in the shower.

CHAPTER 9

As the pair of lovers stepped out of the shower, Bibi ran her left hand along Martin's chest.

"Squeaky clean," she said as she kissed his wet skin.

"That's how I roll," Martin replied as he pushed a strand of wet hair out of her face and kissed her. When they came up for air, Martin pushed a towel at her.

"Dry and clean, if I can," he said with a smirk as he grabbed his own towel.

They toweled themselves off. Bibi walked out of the bathroom and took the suitcases off the bed. Martin looked in the foggy mirror. He grabbed a washcloth and dried it off. He looked at the angry red marks around his throat and swallowed hard.

—*to see them rip the flesh from your bones.*

Hiram's words seemed to hold a special place in his mind, coming forward when least desired.

"Well," Martin whispered at his reflection. "We all gotta go sometime..."

He stepped out of the bathroom and collapsed on the bed. Bibi lay down next to him and stared at the ceiling. She turned her head to look at him. Martin stared straight ahead, his jaw muscle clenching ever so slightly in the dim light of the motel room. She could almost sense the wheels turning in his mind.

"Why me?" she asked.

Martin blinked and looked at her.

"What do you mean?" he asked as he raised his perfectly trimmed eyebrows.

Bibi propped herself up on her right arm stub and looked down at him. "Why do you stay with me?" she asked as she gently touched the curves of his chest and well-toned abs. "I mean, look at you. You can have any woman you want."

"You're right," Martin said as he took her hand in his and brought it to his lips. "And I want you. So, I have you."

"But why do you want me?" she asked and giggled as she pulled her hand away playfully.

Martin turned on his side to face her. She rested back down on the pillow so they were at the same level.

"You calm me," he said as he caressed her cheek and ran his hand down her neck to her chest. "When I'm not with you, I'm jittery, I engage in obsessive, repetitive routines, and I'm genuinely miserable. When I'm with you, I'm not afraid of anything."

He brought his hand to her chin and looked deep into her eyes, his sincerity burning in that fierce but calm gaze. "I feel normal. I am nothing without you, Bibi—a shell of a man going through the motions."

Bibi nodded. "Okay. I'm just glad to hear it's not because you have an amputee fetish."

Martin gave her a wicked grin. "Well, I didn't say I didn't have that..."

"You little—" Bibi shouted as she grabbed at him.

Martin took her arm and pulled her towards him. They wrestled playfully on the bed for several minutes. Finally, Martin lay on his back with his hands in the air.

"I surrender!" he exclaimed, laughing.

Bibi ceased her playful attack and lay down on her back. "You've already won," she whispered.

Martin moved over to her and rested his head on her chest. She caressed his slightly damp hair and Martin drifted off to sleep.

"I want to spend my forever with you," she whispered as she closed her eyes and found her own slumber.

Outside the motel, Hiram sat still as death in the stale darkness, reflecting on his new undead existence. He held his hand up in front of his face, barely able to make out the grey appendage in the sparse light coming from the motel office window. He moved the fingers and shook his head.

"Everything should fall to silence and decay, yet here I am experiencing the strange wonder of magic. Neurons somehow still fire in a dead brain. Mysterious mystical signals travel a decaying network of nerves to make everything move."

He dropped his hand into his lap and lay his head back on the headrest. "Thoughts are still here, but the emotion... seems to have disappeared. My unquenchable desire for killing now focused only on this one quarry. What happens when the others finally get to him and pull him to pieces? I'll have my delight. I think I can still feel that, but what then? What will this existence bring? Maybe I'll find my final rest... or maybe I won't. Curious."

A slight buzzing sound drew his attention to a single

fly landing on his nose. Another landed on his sleeve. He swung his arm at them and they buzzed away, but then came back along with three more. A line of the flies started trickling in through the open window.

"Oh joy. Cadaver flies."

Hiram swatted at the flies as they landed, smashing them in little goopy starbursts on his clothing.

Martin woke up to a dark room and smiled. A hand that wasn't his grasped his manhood.

"Oh baby, that feels so good," Martin moaned. He looked over at Bibi and saw she was still asleep and not touching him. He jerked the covers off and screamed when he saw the disembodied zombie hand grasping his tool.

Martin bolted up awake in a no longer dark room with early morning sunlight piercing the cheap motel curtains.

"Fuck!" Martin screamed as he put his hands on his face, the sheets and bedspread still covering his body.

Bibi stirred next to him and frowned. "What's wrong?" she asked as she tried to blink the sleep out of her eyes.

"Nothing. Thought I was getting a hand job."

Bibi perked up. "Oh, you want one?"

"No!" Martin shouted, and then held up his hand. "Sorry, no, I wasn't getting one from you in the nightmare. Maybe we should just let it alone."

Bibi raised the covers up and saw Martin's member was at full staff. She looked at Martin with a grin. "Maybe we can try something else."

Bibi climbed on top of Martin and they began having slow and sensual sex. As Martin reached his hand to cup Bibi's breast, he heard the door handle jiggling and looked toward the door.

"Someone's trying to get in. Dammit, Hiram!" Martin shouted as Bibi climbed off him. Martin pulled on a pair of pants while Bibi quickly strapped on her prosthetic arm and pulled on a shirt and panties.

"Shit!" Bibi cried out. "That fucking asshole."

Bibi grabbed her machete as Martin walked over to the door. He looked through the peephole but saw nothing.

"What the fuck?" he murmured as he pulled the door open, keeping his eye on the parking lot outside. Below his line of sight, the disembodied zombie arm hung onto the door handle. As it passed by Martin's waist, it let go of the handle and grabbed onto Martin's pants, grasping the waistline.

"Dammit!" Martin shouted as Bibi screamed. Martin whirled around, but the undead hand had a death grip on his pants. He reached around to grab it, but couldn't seem to grasp the slippery undead flesh. Bibi grabbed her towel from the night before and wrapped it around the arm. She pulled and detached it from Martin's waistband. She flung it into the bathtub. The arm flopped around angrily as it tried to grab the slick surface of the porcelain.

Martin walked into the bathroom and cocked his head at the arm flopping around. His eyes went wide as he realized the hand in the tub was missing the middle finger. He ran out of the bathroom, tugged his pants down and climbed on the bed with his ass sticking out at Bibi.

"Get it out!" he screamed. "Get it out!"

It took Bibi a moment to realize what Martin meant as her eyes landed on the severed end of a finger sticking out of his anus. She grabbed a pillow and pulled the pillow case off it. She pushed the pillow case between Martin's butt cheeks to get a grasp on the severed finger.

"It's worming its way in!" Martin screamed.

The motel clerk appeared at the door to see what all the yelling was about. His jaw dropped open as he saw Bibi tugging at Martin's ass with a pillow case.

"Push!" Bibi screamed.

Martin grunted a few times, straining until his face turned red. Bibi grabbed the offending digit with both hands and pulled.

"What the fuck?" the motel clerk finally shouted.

"Could we have a little fucking privacy, please?" Bibi shouted back at him.

The motel clerk blinked his eyes and instinctively pulled the door shut. He grimaced and looked down at his hand. There was some kind of gross, sticky fluid on the handle. He gagged and ran for his office.

Bibi finally pulled the wriggling finger from Martin's ass. She ran into the bathroom, dumped it into the toilet and flushed it away.

Martin limped into the bathroom and grabbed a washcloth. He got it wet, lathered it up, and then frantically scrubbed his ass clean. Bibi just stood there in shock as she stared at the refilling toilet bowl. Martin finally stopped scrubbing and rinsed the washcloth. He gingerly wiped the remaining soap residue from his raw anus.

"Jesus," Martin said with a sigh. Bibi looked up at him and just shook her head.

"That was messed up," Bibi whispered.

"Yeah," Martin said as he nodded his head. He wiggled his butt just to make sure there wasn't a small piece of zombie still stuck up inside him.

As they fell silent, the rhythmic thumping of the disembodied zombie arm flopping around in the bathtub caused them both to look at it. They looked at each other and then back down at the angry limb.

"Think we should hit the road before we get more visitors," Bibi said.

"Yeah," Martin responded as Bibi walked out of the bathroom past him. She finished getting dressed as Martin walked gingerly out of the bathroom. Bibi saw him wincing and sighed.

"Maybe I should drive?" she asked.

"Yeah," Martin said mechanically as he pulled on the rest of his clothes. He got dressed in a kind of mental fog as the thought of what that finger might have done if it had gotten inside him wandered through his mind. His imagination ran wild with visions of his bowels being expelled through his ass and punctured holes in his abdomen. He felt he'd probably fall down in agony and just lie there screaming as the zombie finger did its worst to his insides, bleeding to death on the ratty motel carpet.

Bibi grabbed his face with both hands. "Martin!" she shouted. He blinked and looked at her. "It's going to be all right. We just need to go," Bibi said. She ran her fingers through his hair gently. "Okay?"

"Yeah," Martin said, as he nodded his head and sniffed. "Fuck, yeah, let's go."

He seemed to be back in control as he pulled on one of his shoes. He grimaced and dropped the shoe. "I'll get a new pair from the trunk," Martin said. He picked up the suitcases and Bibi walked out the door with him. Martin popped the trunk open.

"Morning, *vato!*" Hector said in a muted voice.

"Shut up!" Martin shouted at him as he put the suitcases in. He looked around the parking lot for any more surprises as he slid on a new pair of shoes.

Martin and Bibi got in the car and immediately wrinkled their noses. They looked at Hiram in the back seat. He looked back at them with a big smile. Smashed flies peppered his clothing.

"You knew that arm was hanging there, didn't you?" Martin asked him.

"Martin," Hiram replied calmly. "I'm not here to save your life. I'm here to watch you die."

Martin clenched his jaw. "So why didn't you come watch?" he asked.

"Honestly, Martin, it was only one arm. It would not kill you all by itself. Just give you a little trouble, which it sounds like it did." Hiram chuckled. "And that's all right by me."

"Martin, I'm chopping him up when we get to Area 51," Bibi announced. "Then I'm going to burn his little zombie pieces in a bonfire."

"Works for me," Martin replied as Bibi started the car.

"Pansies," Hiram replied.

"I love what you've done with your wardrobe, Hiram," Bibi said as she smiled at him. "The dead flies seem a bold yet fitting fashion statement."

Bibi backed out and turned around in the parking lot. She drove quickly past the motel office as the clerk came out and watched them drive away. The clerk scratched his head and then looked at their motel room. They'd left the door wide open with the small garbage bag still next to the door.

He looked back at the driveway to the motel and didn't see them coming back.

"Huh," he murmured. He walked toward the now empty motel room, but stopped in the middle of the pavement and looked down at his hand. After gagging, he hurried back into the office, returning with a rag and a spray bottle of cleaner.

He walked to the door, looked at the bag, and tapped it tentatively with his foot.

"Well, at least they cleaned up," he said. Quickly spraying the door handle, he wiped it aggressively with the rag. In the morning light, it seemed to have cleaned the mysterious substance off the surface. With a sigh, he rubbed his eyes and shrugged his shoulders.

Inside the room, next to the bathroom door, the clerk found a pair of tennis shoes. After a brief inspection of the footwear, he couldn't identify the substance on the surface of the shoes and wrinkled his nose at the unusually foul smell.

"What did he step in?" the clerk asked. At that moment, a wet flop came from the bathroom and he noticed the disembodied arm crawling across the stained linoleum toward him. He stood up, backed up into the bed, pissed his pants and fainted. As he fell backward onto the bed, a dark spot spread across the crotch of his khaki pants.

The zombie arm simply dragged itself past the unconscious clerk and made its way out the motel room door.

CHAPTER 10

As they passed a sign showing Las Vegas twenty miles away, Martin turned on the radio. He switched the channels looking for some news about zombies in Los Angeles, but there was nothing, not a peep about the undead roaming the streets. He looked over at Bibi as she drove in silence.

"The zombies were all over the streets last night. Surely someone must've seen them and said something," Martin said.

"Government probably suppressed it." Hiram said. Martin turned to look at him. "Total news blackout. They probably gathered all the zombies and zombie pieces into shipping containers and sunk them to the bottom of the ocean. Gathered the people who were eyewitnesses and told them they'd been hallucinating or something. Hell, they probably shot them up with drugs to make them forget."

"Come on, that doesn't happen," Martin replied.

"The cat was already out of the bag when they found your latest kill, junior. That's why the Handyman Killer was all over the headlines," Hiram said as he looked out the window. "This patch of dirt seems familiar."

"Wait," Bibi said, looking at Martin. "You're the Handyman Killer?"

"I didn't pick the name," Martin said as he turned back in his seat to look at the long road ahead of them. "But, yeah. That's me."

"Wow," Bibi said in awe. "You're so brave!"

"Brave?" Martin asked.

"Damn right!" Bibi replied. "When I think of how many people I wanted to kill over the last ten years, some of them still really deserved it—but I just couldn't face the consequences. But you? You said 'Fuck it! Die asshole!'"

"Huh," Martin said and nodded his head. "I guess I did."

Bibi spotted a gas station ahead and looked down at the gas gauge. "We could use some gas," she said. She glanced at the back seat and wrinkled her nose. "And maybe a few other things."

Bibi pulled up to the pumps. She and Martin both got out.

Martin whipped out two credit cards. "I got this. You get supplies," he said and tossed one card to her. She caught it with one hand, never breaking stride as she walked into the store.

Hiram watched her enter the building as Martin pulled the nozzle off the pump and stuck it into the gas tank. "She's gonna die, ya know," Hiram said. Martin looked at Hiram and then glanced at the store.

"Probably," Martin said with a sigh. "There's no way I could talk her out of it and it just might be better this way."

Hiram began singing "You Always Hurt The One You Love."

Martin slapped the side of the car. "Shut up."

"There's always a critic," Hiram murmured.

After a few minutes, Bibi exited the store with a bag full of stuff. She set the bag down on the passenger seat and opened it. She pulled out a container of disinfectant wipes, popped it open, and pulled a few out. She then pulled the seat forward and began cleaning the flies off of Hiram.

"Oh, to what do I owe the pleasure of a sponge bath?" Hiram asked with a smirch.

"You know," Bibi said as she methodically picked the dead insects from Hiram's clothing. "I could just cutoff your arms, shove a baseball in your mouth and duct tape your face shut."

"Your charms know no bounds," Hiram replied.

Martin finished with the pump and poked his head in the driver's side window. "You sure it's worth the trouble?" he asked.

Bibi finished cleaning off the flies and grabbed one of dozens of cardboard air fresheners. She ripped the package open and affixed the freshener to Hiram's clothing.

"If I could smell, I'm sure I'd be disturbed," Hiram mused.

"We gotta drive through Vegas with stinky britches here," Bibi said. "Don't want to get pulled over for creating a public nuisance."

"Sorry, my decomposing gases are leaking out through the hole your boyfriend made in me."

"I'll just be glad when we're rid of your sorry, stinky ass," Bibi sniped back as she continued the laborious process of tying air fresheners to their back seat passenger. "I'd tell you to bite me, but I'm afraid you'd actually do it."

"You talk to your mother like that?" Hiram said as Bibi finished tying the last dog shaped cardboard cutout to the buttons on his suit coat.

"Dialog with mom was limited to me saying nothing to her and her saying something like—'Bibi, bring me another beer' or maybe 'come back to bed, your stepfather misses you.'" Bibi shoved the seat back into place and walked back around the car to the driver's side. She paused at the car door, her hand inches from the door handle as she stared at the convenience store.

A police car pulled up right by the store. An officer got out of the car and glanced her way. He gave her a nod and a smile. He walked into the store and Bibi realized she'd been holding her breath and let it out in a gasp. She quickly climbed into the car and started it up. She drove off slowly, even though she desperately wanted to slam her foot to the floor and burn rubber leaving the area.

As the policeman walked out of the store, he stopped suddenly and wrinkled his nose. He looked around briefly and then raised his arm and sniffed his under arm. He shook his head and got back in his car.

"What if he checks our plate?" Bibi asked as she drove back onto the highway. There didn't appear to be any other cars on the road at this early hour.

"It won't come back to me," Martin said. "I keep the plates rotated to drivers outside the county limits."

"Smart," Hiram said. "I'm surprised anyone picked up on your trail at all."

"Well, I think you had something to do with that,"

Martin replied. "That little stunt you pulled on the television, the anonymous tip, was enough to get them wondering. Somehow, they got pointed in my direction."

"Well, it was personal, not business, so..."

"What is that?" Bibi asked as she pointed ahead of them. A lone figure stood in the road. As they got closer, Martin grunted.

"Well, if it's a zombie, it's not one of mine," Martin said. "I didn't dump anyone out this far."

Hiram leaned forward and peered at the approaching figure. "Hard to tell, but I was pretty prolific, and the desert was a favorite dumping ground. Police usually just found bones, but this one seems to have some meat on him still. Could be Doctor Tang, a virologist who was a patient of mine ten years ago. Perfect nose–took me a while to catch up to him after that many years."

"If he had a perfect nose, why did he come to see you?"

"Scar on his chin from a childhood accident. Got it smoothed out until it was nearly invisible. He could make it disappear completely with a light touch of foundation. Vainest virologist I ever met and I'm counting all the women," Hiram sat back in the seat.

As they got closer, the zombie changed its movements, trying to intercept the car as it approached.

"Try to go around it. They're not quick," Martin said. Bibi nodded and made a swerve around the undead as she came to it. The zombie leapt through the air and crashed through the windshield, hands slipping into place around Martin's neck. It attempted to pull its face toward Martin to bite him as well.

Hiram leaned forward as Bibi tried to get control of the car and pull over. "Both hands and no nose," Hiram said as he examined the face of the zombie trying to eat Martin. "Gotta be the doc."

Hiram then sat back and watched contentedly as the zombie continued its attack. Bibi pulled the car to the side of the road. She ran to the trunk and popped it open.

"Fuck!" she hissed as she pulled her suitcase toward her and unlatched it.

"Hey, pretty lady!" Hector called out from his jar. Bibi jumped and looked down to the right, seeing the head in the jar for the first time.

"What the fuck?" Bibi whispered.

"Want a little head?!" Hector shouted and then laughed hysterically.

"Shit!" Bibi shouted as she heard Martin let out a strangled raspy cough. She found her machete and ran to the passenger side. She opened the door.

"Get out so we can kill this thing!" Bibi shouted.

Martin struggled to breathe and talk as he was trying to stop the zombie from strangling him and biting him. "I'm trying," he said in a coarse whisper.

Bibi grabbed the zombie's hair to pull it out of the car. She came back with a fist full of hair and some decaying scalp flesh. She gagged briefly and dropped the amalgam of flesh and hair to the ground. Next, she grabbed the collar of the shirt the zombie wore and tugged on it, but the zombie was firmly implanted in the windshield. She tried with both hands before giving up.

"I can't get him to budge," Bibi stated. She looked at their back seat passenger. "Hiram, can you give us a hand here?"

Hiram clapped his hands together and grinned at her. "Or would you prefer a high five?" he asked smugly.

Martin slipped a little way out of the car, his lower half still stuck in the car. One zombie hand grabbed Martin's shirt and twisted it while the other hand pressed into his windpipe. It choked him so hard he saw stars. Martin motioned to Bibi, but she shook her head, confused.

"I don't understand? What do you want me to do?" Bibi asked.

"Chop... chop..." Martin gasped.

"Oh," Bibi replied. She started hacking away at the zombie's left arm, staying clear of Martin's arms as he tried to hold off the zombie.

"If you ever need work," Hiram remarked. "You could always get a job with a butcher."

Bibi growled at Hiram, but didn't look at him. She finished chopping through the left arm, but the disembodied arm still grasped Martin's throat. Bibi dropped the machete and grabbed the arm with both of her hands and pulled. She got it off Martin and threw it several feet away.

"Thank you. *Ahhh!*" Martin said and then screamed. The zombie sunk its teeth into his right arm.

"Shit," Bibi groaned. She picked her machete back up and hacked away at the neck of the zombie. With a few swings, she detached the head from the body, but it held Martin firmly in its jaw. His hand dropped with the zombie head still attached to his flesh.

"Gah!" Martin groaned. "This thing won't let go!"

Martin was now half out of the car, his shirt collar held tightly by the zombie's right arm and body, a zombie head biting into his right arm, and his feet struggled to give him enough leverage to pull himself completely out of the car.

"What now?" Bibi asked, the exasperation rising in her voice. Her face was red from exertion and the rising desert heat.

"Chop him in half so I can get out of the car!" Martin shouted.

"Oh, I wouldn't recommend that," Hiram said with a chuckle.

"Shut the fuck up!" Bibi shouted at Hiram. She hacked away at the zombie's back, trying to sever the spine to cut the zombie in half. After a few minutes, she reached a critical point and finally cut through the spine. Martin and the top half of the zombie fell out of the car. The zombie's bloated belly burst open with a sickening pop upon impact and noxious juices spilled forth, covering Martin's lower half.

"Oh no..." Martin groaned before he and Bibi spontaneously vomited from the smell of the decomposed flesh and juices spilled out all around them. The zombie continued to grasp at Martin's shirt as he pulled himself away from the spreading puddle, his right arm still impaired by the severed zombie head attached to it.

Bibi was so overwhelmed, she held onto the car for balance as she puked repeatedly until she began dry heaving. Next to her hand, the legs of the zombie's lower half thrashed on the hood as it tried to extricate itself from the jagged edges of the windshield. Hiram watched the entire scene with a gleam in his eye, looking back and forth between Bibi and Martin as they struggled to defeat the zombie.

"This is worth the price of admission right here," he said with a giggle.

Martin wrenched the zombie's right hand off his collar and pushed the torso away from him. He laid his right arm on the ground with the zombie head still biting into it. He took a blade from his back sheath and stabbed the zombie's head through the jaw. Prying the blade down, he broke the lower jaw off the head, freeing his right arm. He scrambled backward to sit against the back tire of the car, cradling his bleeding right arm.

"Bibi," Martin gasped. "Grab the medical kit from the trunk."

Bibi wiped the puke from her jaw with her sleeve and ran back to the open trunk. Hector smiled when he saw her again through the jar. His muffled voice greeted her as she looked for the kit.

"Hey baby," his muffled voice shouted. "Want to hook up after I kill your boyfriend? You can just put me between your legs!"

Hector pushed his tongue out in a pantomime.

"Yuck!" Bibi replied as she glanced his way. She finally located the kit and disappeared from Hector's view.

"Aww, don't play hard to get! Man, just when I thought I was getting lucky," Hector said and then laughed maniacally.

"Got it!" she told Martin.

"Just hand it here," Martin said as he stretched out his left hand. "I know the smell is horrible."

"It's okay," Bibi replied. "I don't think I have anything left to vomit."

Sticking his head around the small half window, Hiram

watched them and laughed.

Bibi glared at him. "What are you laughing at, asshole?" she screamed at him.

"That was only one zombie!" Hiram shouted and then disappeared from view, laughing hysterically.

Bibi was stunned for a moment as she realized just how true Hiram's statement was. She looked at Martin with fresh worry in her eyes. Shaking her head, she helped pour hydrogen peroxide on the wound; he grimaced as it dripped onto the bloody bite mark and bubbled. After a minute or two, he shook his arm off, and she helped him wrap the wound with a bandage and taped it into place. He rested his head against the car again. Bibi looked down at the carnage of the shredded zombie. The torso with one arm tried to drag itself toward Martin, the head with dead eyes looked around trying to find its prey and the legs wiggled on the hood of the car. Bibi sighed, picked up the kit, walked around to the trunk, almost in a daze, and put the kit back. Her eyes locked on Hector.

"I know you're thinking about it, baby!" he shouted and stuck his tongue out again.

Bibi groaned and slammed the trunk. She walked back around to Martin and picked up her machete. It dripped with slime. She gagged for a moment and then shook the weapon off.

Martin looked up at a sign for the next exit advertising a car wash. He got up and smiled at Bibi.

"You drive alongside. We're gonna get washed up," he said as he pointed to the sign and began walking up the road. He kicked at the lone zombie arm trying to grab him. He took hold of one of the zombie legs stuck in the windshield and pulled the entire bottom half off the car onto the ground, leaving a path of rotted entrails behind on the dash and hood. Martin turned away and threw up again.

The zombie legs gyrated madly on the ground as they tried to get some kind of purchase to stand up. Bibi pulled the rest of the shattered windshield off the car, climbed in, and drove slowly beside Martin.

"Well, I don't know about you two, but I think this is pretty fucking exciting!" Hiram said as he leaned forward. Bibi glared at him.

Bibi kept pace with Martin on the curiously quiet highway. A few minutes later, she pulled into the parking lot of the gas station with the attached automated car wash. Martin walked up to the kiosk. He pulled out his wallet and took out the credit card he'd just used to pay for gas. He purchased the wash and put his card back in the wallet, which he then set on top of the kiosk. He quickly stripped off all his clothes and tossed them off to the side as Bibi drove into the car wash.

"Close your eyes and breathe through your nose if you can," Martin advised before he took his position, naked and barefoot, walking behind the car into the spray of water and soap.

After the first couple of passes, Bibi put her hands over her face to reduce the strength of the water spray. The interior of the muscle car was drenched by the time they got through the wash. Bibi pulled over to a standalone car vacuum and got out. Water spilled from the interior.

"I've never felt so clean," Hiram quipped from the back seat.

Martin, his skin red from the beat of the high pressure

spray, walked to the trunk and popped it open.

"Hey *vato!* Did you wash up before lunch? You look good enough to eat!" Hector shouted from his jar.

Martin sighed and got another set of clothing from his reserves. He dressed quickly.

"I like my meat with dressing!" Hector called out.

Martin shut the trunk without acknowledging the disembodied head's comment.

Back on the highway, the police officer from the other convenience store passed the location of the zombie assault. He quickly pulled over just past the carnage that lay on the side of the road. As he walked back to the one armed, headless torso, it dragged itself in his direction. His fingers pinched his nose as the pungent aroma of the dead drifted through the air. A few feet behind the torso, he spotted a disembodied head trying to move its broken jaw, and an arm flopped on the hot pavement all by itself. A pair of legs and lower torso got up on its knees and stood up, unsteadily stumbling toward him.

"What the hell?" the officer whispered as he looked out into the road to see if any traffic was close. There was nothing for miles in both directions. He stepped out into the road way as the legs walked by him, continuing their eastward trajectory.

The officer stayed parallel with the legs as they made their way past his vehicle. Satisfied they weren't after him, he climbed into his car and got on the radio. "This is Officer Billings. I've got a situation."

"This is dispatch. Officer Billings, can you repeat?"

"There's a... dead body. Half of it is walking around

and the other half is crawling." The officer watched the legs continue walking down the road away from him toward a gas station off in the distance.

"Dan," came another voice back. "This is Sheriff Hathaway. Do not engage the body parts. There's a cleanup crew on the way."

"A cleanup crew? We have to gather evidence! Someone died..." His voice trailed off as he looked in his passenger side mirror and saw the torso moving in the distance. "I think..."

"We've been advised to leave it alone. Orders from higher up."

"There was a car that drove by, maroon Dodge Charger I think, I could—"

"Do not engage the Charger or its occupants. Orders from higher up."

Officer Billings frowned. "Orders from who, Bill?" he asked.

"I don't like it anymore than you do, Dan. I'm just following orders. I can't say anymore."

Officer Billings put the radio back on the clip. "This is bullshit," he announced. He looked around and sighed.

Martin opened the passenger side door and let the water drain out. He paid for the car vacuum and sucked the water off the car's floorboards. The vacuum whined in protest, but continued functioning. He walked around to Bibi's side and did the same thing. After he got most of the water out, the vacuum screeched and a puff of smoke erupted from the machine. Martin dropped the hose and got back in on the passenger side. He sat down with a squish. Bibi climbed in and sat down with a squish as well. She was soaked to the bone. Martin looked over at her and smiled.

"Can I show you a good time, or what, baby?!" he said. Bibi smiled, and they both laughed as she started the car and drove away from the car wash. Hiram looked at them both and just shook his head.

CHAPTER 11

As they continued down the interstate highway, the buildings of the Vegas strip loomed in the distance. Martin pointed ahead and shouted through the wind coming in through the open windshield.

"Just continue through on—"

"I know how to get there!" Bibi shouted back testily.

Martin looked at her with raised eyebrows. She glanced at him and grimaced. "Care to elaborate?" Martin asked.

"We'll stop at the Crimson Motor Cafe just east of town for brunch. I'll explain then," she shouted back.

"Splendid!" Hiram shouted from the back seat. Martin looked back at him and saw the air fresheners flopping about madly in the wind. Martin turned back to look at the city growing larger by the minute.

The drive by the Strip and downtown Las Vegas was uneventful. It was early morning, so the flurry of activity was at a minimum. The tall buildings with the flashy exteriors were muted during the day. They really came alive when the sun went down. There were only a few cars on the highway, but few people gave the battered vehicle more than a passing glance. More than once, though, they passed a police vehicle and were increasingly amazed none pursued them.

As they got past the 599 loop, Bibi headed for the next exit and got off at the Las Vegas Motor Speedway exit. Just off the exit, she pulled into a small café with a single car in the parking lot. She parked across the parking lot a suitable distance from the entrance.

"Fewer casual prying eyes out here," she said as she put the car in park.

Martin looked around and held up his hands. "How did you know this was here?" he asked.

Bibi sighed. "I grew up in Henderson. My mother is still here." She said the word 'mother' like it was poison.

Martin looked at the restaurant. "At the Crimson Motor Café?" he asked.

"Lord no," Bibi replied. "She works at a strip club just a little further north. Mostly caters to the locals."

"Your mom's a stripper?" Hiram asked.

"She's the manager, asshole," she said as she scowled at Hiram. "I sure as hell wouldn't want to see her naked."

She looked back at Martin. "Can we just go in and get some food? I'd like to chat far away from the freeloading scum we're carting around."

"Touchy," Hiram said with a smirk.

"Sure," Martin replied as he got out. He stopped and peered back at Hiram. "Any fresh victims around here?"

"Sadly, no," Hiram replied. "We're much too close to town for a body dump."

"Yeah," Martin replied. "That's what I figured too."

Martin closed the door and headed toward the

restaurant, holding his hand out for Bibi to grab as she joined him.

"Have you dried off?" Martin asked.

"Mostly," Bibi replied. "But I'd still like to change my clothes. My under things are still moist and sticking to me."

"Why don't you grab something to change into? You can use the bathroom here," Martin said.

"Be right back," Bibi said with a smile.

She ran back to the car and popped open the trunk. Martin watched her every move and felt a thrill in his heart. She didn't just make him feel safe, she made him *feel*. He'd been wandering through a desert void of any genuine emotion before she'd come into his life. He felt a pang of regret about bringing her along on this likely fatal road trip.

She quickly returned with a handful of clothing. They walked into the café, found a seat, and then she disappeared with the clothing into the bathroom. After a few minutes, the waitress walked up with a coffee pot in hand.

"Coffee?" she asked. Martin looked up and noticed the pregnant brunette waitress had a name tag that read Anna. Martin looked to his left and saw two coffee cups upside down on two small plates. He turned them both over and set them on the edge of the table near the waitress.

"That would be great, Anna. Thank you," Martin replied. Anna smiled briefly and filled the cups with the steaming brew.

Bibi emerged from the bathroom and hastened to the booth Martin sat in. She carried a trash bag that Martin assumed contained the wet clothing she'd just changed out of. The waitress looked up at Bibi and sighed.

"Bibi," the waitress said curtly.

"Anna," Bibi replied as she tossed the bag on top of the booth bench against the wall.

The waitress turned to go.

"How's Mom?" Bibi asked. The waitress stopped and took a deep breath before turning around.

"I wouldn't know," Anna replied.

"Have a falling out?" Bibi said with a smile.

"Phyllis is still Phyllis as far as I know," Anna said as she walked away.

Martin's jaw hung open. He turned to look at the back of the retreating waitress and then back at Bibi.

"Is she your sister? You never told me you had any family before today," Martin said.

"I don't," Bibi replied as she reached over to get a menu from the little stand against the wall. "I have physical relatives. They haven't been family for a long time."

"You're from here. That's why you know your way around."

Bibi nodded. She looked at the menu and then glanced at where Anna had disappeared. "I have wonderful memories of the raceway. My father was a mechanic and an amateur driver. We used to come out here all the time."

Martin glanced out at his battered car sitting in the parking lot. "Well, I could use a talented mechanic, but maybe we should contact a body repair specialist first," Martin said with a smirk.

Bibi glanced out at the car. "Just some dents we can probably pound out and buff. I know..." Bibi stopped herself and swallowed. "I knew a guy."

Anna returned with a small notepad. "Can I take your order?" she asked.

"How far along are you?" Bibi asked. Anna dropped her arm and leaned against the back of Martin's bench seat.

"Are we really gonna do this?" Anna asked.

"Look, you're my sister, so," Bibi said with a shrug.

"Sister... sure," Anna replied with venom. "Seven months, if you really need to know."

"Okay. You excited?" Bibi asked.

"No," Ann replied sharply. She raised the notepad back up and pulled out a pen. "Your order?

Martin glanced at the notepad and noticed the red rings around Anna's wrists.

"What happened to your wrists?" he asked.

"Jesus," Anna said, exasperated. "Can we just leave it alone?"

Bibi sat down in her seat finally and set the menu down. She looked at Anna and raised an eyebrow. "Who's the father?" Bibi asked. Tears welled up in Anna's eyes. "Shit, Anna, no..."

"What the fuck did you think that asshole was going to do when his prize ran away, Bibi? Two fucking years I had to fight him off," Anna screamed. The cook stepped out from the kitchen and watched them from afar.

"You should've moved out," Bibi replied, stone faced.

"I fucking did," Anna replied. She held up her wrist. "Derek fucking kidnapped me and raped me in his cabin in Tahoe for weeks. They fucking kept me there for six months while this thing grew inside me."

Bibi dropped her mouth open and then looked down.

The table in front of her got blurry as she fought off her own tears.

"Cops fucking shot him, so at least the asshole's dead," Anna continued. "I have to carry this thing to term since I can't abort it now. Oh, and Phyllis got off scot-free because they couldn't find any evidence. It's been a really exceptional year."

"I'm sorry, I didn't know," Bibi replied in a subdued whisper.

"Well, now you fucking do," Anna replied. "Now, can I take your fucking order or what?"

"Breakfast special would be great," Martin replied. Bibi looked up at him with tears in her eyes. "Two please. Thanks."

Anna scribbled on the notepad. "You're welcome," she said and walked away toward the kitchen counter.

"Catching up with family is always fun," Martin replied. "Good choice for a meal stop."

"I didn't know she worked here," Bibi replied as she wiped the tears from her face. "Davis Grant must've taken pity on her. He was a good friend of Dad's before he retired from racing and took over this place. That's the only reason I came here."

"You're not going to stop by and see your mom?"

"Hell no," Bibi said. "While I was 'enjoying' my own special time with that asshole Derek, Phyllis ran interference for him. She forced me to cleanse myself before I left the house so there wouldn't be any forensic evidence to corroborate the abuse. It doesn't surprise me she helped that asshole rape Anna. There's a fresh place in hell for her."

"Want me to kill her on our way through?" Martin asked as he sipped his coffee. Bibi smiled and wiped her tears away.

"No, but that's sweet of you to offer," she said with a sigh. She took a drink of coffee and let the hot liquid burn on its way down. "I'd like to have that honor if the opportunity presents itself. She won't be there for hours, though, and I think we have more pressing matters."

"About that," Martin said as he leaned forward. "I'm not certain we'll make it out of Area 51 alive. It's a fool's errand to head to them, anyway. I just couldn't think of anyone else who might be equipped to deal with the army of undead coming after me. You could stay back with your sister and help her with the baby."

"Umm," Bibi said. "I went to the police. They didn't believe me. Mom and Derek called me a liar and Anna had been untouched to that point, so she called me a liar, as well. I didn't think the asshole would go after her. I thought he had a thing for blondes. So, I blame myself a bit for her predicament. I should've at least tried to take her with me."

"What he did wasn't your fault," Martin replied.

"I was jealous of her because she wasn't getting the 'attention' from Derek that I was. She got to have a normal childhood. We didn't part on the best of terms. I'm not proud of it, but when I left, I secretly wished she would suffer just a little like I had. I'm no saint, Martin."

"Look, the real asshole is dead. That really just leaves your mom, but at least she's not a part of either of your lives anymore."

"Small consolation that she doesn't have any more

kids to offer to potential suitors," Bibi said. "So, at least she'll die alone and miserable. Tiny victories, I guess."

Anna returned with their meals. She set them down on the table.

"Hey," Bibi said to her. Anna looked at her with a glare. "I'm sorry for leaving you to that monster. If I'm still alive in a few days, I'd like to come back and help. I'll even go with you to drop the little bastard off at CPS."

Anna pinched her lips together and took a deep breath. She simply nodded and walked away.

They both felt the urgency of their hunger rise and stopped talking to consume the food Anna had brought.

Detective Johnson watched the army personnel securing straps to the large cargo container. The whirring beat of the twin set of blades from a heavy lift helicopter overhead accompanied the shouts of the soldiers rushing around. A firm downdraft pushed dust and debris away from the container. Detective Smithers wrinkled his nose.

"They still smell bad, even locked in that container," the younger detective stated.

"It's not like they can wrap them in body bags," Detective Johnson replied as he took a small amount of ointment from a container and wiped it under his nose. "You want some of this? The menthol really cuts the odor."

Detective Smithers shook his head as he pressed a hand against his back.

"I think the only thing I need is a back rub, a heating pad, and some sleep. I hate all nighters," he replied as he then adjusted his shoulders. "How many times has the government shut down a serial killer investigation on you like this?"

"Never in my thirty years on the force," Detective Johnson said. A shout brought his attention to their left, where Agent Jansen yelled animatedly at an Army Captain who held his hands out to prevent any movement toward the container. The agent threw his notepad on the ground and turned away from the officer while he shouted obscenities into the air.

"Well," Detective Johnson said. "At least Jansen's taking it well."

"I wonder if he had to sign an NDA?" Detective Smithers mused.

"I'm sure he sees plenty of stuff he's not supposed to talk about every day," Detective Johnson replied. "Although, I'd guess zombies mixed in with a serial killer is a first."

A clinking sound brought the duo's attention back to the cargo container as it slowly rose off the ground. It went up a few hundred feet and then moved off into the distance, heading east toward the desert.

"What do you think they're going to do with them?" Detective Smithers asked.

"I don't really care. We got the DNA off the arms in the warehouse and the twenty bodies we found, so we can use to that to close most of those missing persons cases. After and if they return those samples to us, that is."

"But there were way more than just those arms' worth of zombies. Where do you suppose the others came from?"

Detective Johnson waited until the helicopter completely disappeared and then turned around.

"Well, if they keep their word and send us samples from all of them, once they've 'become inanimate,' whatever that means, then we can figure that out. Maybe there's more than one killer out there with reanimated victims," Detective Johnson walked toward their unmarked police car.

"Maybe we'll be luckier if we don't get those samples back," Detective Smithers said. "Can you imagine the paperwork?"

They both laughed and climbed into their car.

CHAPTER 12

As Bibi and Martin left the restaurant, he squeezed her hand. She looked at him and smiled.

"Would it be okay if I left your sister something to help her get by?"

Bibi furrowed her brows and nodded. "You mean like a bigger tip?" Bibi asked.

"A much bigger tip," Martin replied.

When they got to the car, Martin went to the trunk and grabbed a satchel behind Hector's jar. He set it on the edge of trunk and opened it, revealing multiple stacks of cash. Bibi dropped her jaw open.

"How much is that?"

"Enough for her to get away from here forever," Martin replied. He removed one stack and placed it back behind Hector.

"You trying to sweeten me up, *vato?*" Hector quipped.

"If I wanted to do that," Martin replied. "I'd just add some sugar to the jar."

Martin took the satchel and closed the trunk. "Just wait here," Martin said. "Might be less drama that way."

"Sure," Bibi said.

Martin walked back into the restaurant. Anna was cleaning off the table they had just occupied. The dishes were already gone. She looked up. "Did you want something to go?" she asked.

"I've got something for you," Martin replied and set the satchel on the bench. He opened it up and Anna gasped.

"Are you a bank robber?" she asked as she went a little pale.

"No, I'm a... money manager," Martin replied. "Look, this should allow you to get far away from here and start a new life."

"Ya think?" Anna replied, staring at the stacks of cash in the bag.

"Under all that money are the coordinates to a cache of additional funds," Martin whispered as he looked around at the vacant restaurant. "Wait a few days and go retrieve it. You should have enough to buy some property, go to school, or maybe start a business. Heck, you could probably just live off the funds for a few years and do nothing, if you like."

"Why are you doing this?" Anna asked. Her hands were shaking. Martin took her hands in his.

"My foster siblings didn't make it through the system. I don't have any other family. Bibi is everything to me and, well, I'm not sure either of us will survive the next twenty-four hours. She clearly cares for your well-being, even if she's confused by what happened to her. Just remember, she truly cared for you and never wanted to see you get hurt."

"Umm, thank you," was all Anna could manage.

"Can you leave now? It may get dicey in Nevada tonight."

"Dicey?" Anna looked around at the empty restaurant.

"I don't want to skip out on Davis..."

"Take a cab, get as far away from Nevada as you can, and send him a postcard," Martin replied. "Sounds like he's a good man and he'll understand."

Anna nodded and closed the satchel. She left the cleaning rag on the table and walked out the door, pulling her cell phone from her apron.

Martin looked at the table and back at the door closing behind Anna as she left. He picked up the rag and finished cleaning off the table and arranged the condiments and menu rack centered against the wall. After admiring his work for a moment, he folded up the rag and set it on the corner of the table.

Martin caught a glimpse of Anna climbing into a taxicab just off the parking lot as he exited the restaurant. A brief smile crossed his lips as walked back to the car. Bibi kissed him when he returned.

"You didn't have to do that," she said as she climbed into the driver's seat. Martin walked around the car and climbed in.

"It will be good to see someone come out of this disaster ahead," Martin replied.

"Or without a head," Hiram added from the back seat.

"Missed you too, Hiram," Martin replied.

Bibi started the car, and they left the parking lot quickly. Bibi drove back onto the interstate.

Three blocks away, a man in an army uniform watched through binoculars as the car drove onto the highway. He brought his cell phone to his ear.

"They're heading north on 15. Want me to intercept?"

"No," came the reply. "Follow them at a distance, but

I'm pretty sure they'll take 93 and come to us."

"Should I send another team after the waitress?"

"No. She's of no consequence. You have your orders."

The man in the uniform hung up the phone and climbed into the khaki all-terrain vehicle sitting on the side street. He started it up and drove quickly after Bibi and Martin.

Nearly two hours later, they approached Rachel, Nevada. Bibi looked to her left at a fence off in the distance. She slowed down as a dirt road that lead toward the fence appeared and turned off onto what looked like a well-packed dirt road. A ridge rose behind the fence and shadows on the ridge betrayed movement. The armed guard for Area-51 was active and waiting for any trespassers coming up the road. She drove a few yards up the road and they came to a large sign next to the road.

The red and white sign read: NELLIS BOMBING AND GUNNERY RANGE / RESTRICTED AREA / NO TRESPASSING BEYOND THIS POINT / WARNING U.S. Air Force Installation / PHOTOGRAPHY IS PROHIBITED

"They just don't want us going in there," Hiram remarked. Bibi wrinkled her nose. Hiram's funk had returned. There was only so much air fresheners could do.

"Okay, it's gonna get real hairy here in a few minutes," Martin said. "You can get out and I could drive it from here."

"You could," Bibi said with a smile and then slammed her foot down on the accelerator. "Hold on!"

Dirt and rocks flew out behind the car as the tires spun and then caught, propelling the car forward. They careened down the road toward the chain-link fence and smashed through it, throwing a shower of sparks in the air. Bibi continued to floor it and the car bounced up the hillside and over it. They ran directly into a road block with three black SUVs and a panel van. Twelve armed soldiers leveled rifles at them. Bibi slammed on the brakes. The car skid to a halt in a cloud of dust.

"Looks like we're expected," Hiram said.

"Ya think," Bibi sneered.

Martin climbed out of the car, hands raised. "Take me to your leader," Martin said with a smile.

One of the armed men stepped forward, gun still raised. "You're trespassing on government property. You have exactly thirty seconds to get back in your car and leave before we open fire."

"I have a zombie problem," Martin replied calmly.

"Maybe you need to go to Haiti then," the soldier replied.

"I have a disembodied arm and talking head in my trunk. They are both still very active. Guy in the back seat is a full-on undead zombie. Hiram, why don't you get out of the car and show them there's no heart feelings?"

Hiram pushed the passenger seat forward and climbed out of the car. Several of the soldiers switched their aim to point at him directly. "This is getting really old," Hiram said as he hooked his fingers into his chest, yanked the chest plate off, and held up his somewhat beating heart. Two air fresheners dangled from it. One soldier retched.

"It's an acquired taste," Hiram said as he raised his heart to his lips and gave it a kiss.

The lead soldier's walkie-talkie crackled to life. "Bring them in, Sergeant," the voice commanded. "The car too."

Three soldiers flanked Hiram. He put his heart and chest back into place while the armed men corralled him into a panel van, trying to stay downwind. They took Martin and Bibi to separate SUVs and relieved them of their weapons.

Two of the remaining soldiers approached the car and popped the trunk. They retrieved the burlap sack with the wiggling zombie arm in it and Hector in his jar. They set the sack and Hector on the floor of the van next to Hiram.

"Hey, where did lunch go? I'm dying for some white meat!" Hector shouted.

"And so begins my time in hell," Hiram replied and sat back against the side of the panel van. The soldiers closed the doors and latched them shut.

Martin watched the desert terrain pass by in quiet contemplation. He wondered if he'd made the right decision. Would the military believe him? Could they help him? Would they help him?

And then there was the small matter of being a wanted serial killer. He had to admit Hiram had indeed cemented his revenge. There was no denying Martin would indeed die before too long. If he could manage it, he wanted it to be on his terms, but even that seemed out of his hands now.

With his hands cuffed behind him, it was impossible to sit back comfortably in the seat. With a sigh of resignation, he looked forward at the seat ahead of him and noticed a speck of dirt on the back of the headrest. He grit his teeth as the urgent desire to clean it tried to push every other thought, including survival, out of his mind.

In the SUV behind Martin, the soldier sitting in the

passenger side looked back at Bibi and gave an approving nod. Bibi glared at him.

"What are ya looking at, flyboy?" Bibi hissed. "You don't have a chance in hell of getting any of this."

The soldier quickly turned around and kept his eyes forward. The soldier sitting next to Bibi laughed. "Classic virgin noob," the soldier shouted at the soldier in front of him.

"Whatever," the other soldier replied.

After fifteen minutes of driving through the featureless desert, they arrived at an enormous hangar far away from the other buildings on the site. The vehicles drove in through the open hangar doors and stopped side by side in front of a table with military personnel sitting around it. The man sitting at the center, Air Force General Robert Huckster, wearing his dress blues, stood out in contrast to all the other personnel around him dressed in khakis. He got to his feet, followed by the other personnel.

The soldiers exited the cars, saluted the General and then removed Bibi and Martin from their respective vehicles. General Huckster walked up to them and looked them up and down.

"It seems we apprehended you breaking through the perimeter of our facility," he said as he stopped in front of them and clasped his hands behind his back. "I could just have you shot. I'm well within my rights as base commander to use deadly force to guard this facility. Tell me why I shouldn't."

"I'm being chased by zombies," Martin said with a smile. "I figured you could help."

General Huckster narrowed his eyes at Martin and clenched his jaw just for a moment before he smiled back at Martin.

"We can help," the general replied as he looked down at the ground and nodded for a moment. "But tell me, why are they chasing you in particular, Mr. Simon?"

Martin's jaw dropped open momentarily. "How... You know my name?"

General Huckster nodded gravely. He turned away from the duo and focused his eyes on the back wall. Pausing just for a moment, the officer sniffed and frowned. With a sigh, he shook his head and then nodded. Hands clasped behind his back, he turned back around, his lips a thin gray line across his face.

"We also know these zombies are only chasing you. We want to know why."

"What do we get in return?"

"Well, we can probably protect you better than any other entity on the planet. As I said before, we can help."

"Great," Martin said with a sigh of relief.

"There is our standard non-disclosure agreement you must sign. You're about to enter a top secret facility. We must have some measure of protection."

"Of course," Martin replied with a nod.

"Whatever it takes to save Martin, I'm in," Bibi stated.

"Well, of course you are," General Huckster replied with a grin. He turned his head to the men at the table. "Sergeant, paperwork."

One soldier brought two clipboards.

"Master Sargeant," General Huckster said. "I believe our guests will need their cuffs removed to sign."

The soldier behind Martin stepped forward and unlocked his cuffs, putting the opened restraint devices back on his belt. He looked at another soldier behind Bibi.

"Jackson!" he barked. The soldier jumped a little and slung his weapon over his shoulder. He removed Bibi's restraints.

Able to move freely again, Bibi and Martin signed the paperwork the soldier handed them. After reviewing them carefully, the soldier flipped pages and had the duo initial each page. He looked it over one more time and nodded.

"Everything appears in order, sir," the soldier announced and returned to the table with the paperwork.

"Excellent," General Huckster said and then dropped his smile. "Take them into custody."

The soldiers immediately grabbed them and put the handcuffs back on.

"Wait!" Martin shouted. "You said you were going to help!"

General Huckster chuckled. "Oh, I am helping. Helping the United States government," General Huckster glared at Martin. "I never said I would help you."

The general walked back to the table as he barked out orders.

"Bring the Handyman Killer to the interrogation room." Martin's face went white.

Bibi struggled with the soldiers escorting her into a doorway across the hangar. "You bastard! You said you would help!" she shouted before disappearing from view. Martin gave much less resistance to being dragged off; it seemed as though the fight had been drained out of him.

A tow truck arrived in the hangar with Martin's car behind it. Several technicians from the far side of the building converged on the vehicle and readied it for inspection and dissection.

Several lab technicians in white coats approached the

panel van and opened the back while soldiers stood at the ready behind them, rifles raised. Hiram waved at them. They stopped and looked at him in confusion.

"This one is lucid. What do we do with him?" One technician asked another.

"Just put him in the room with the others. We'll deal with him later," came the uninterested reply.

"Fantastic," Hiram said, causing the first technician to do a double take.

"Right, put him in the room with the others," he repeated and led Hiram to the far side of the hangar where the door was marked with biohazard symbols. Another technician grabbed Hector's jar.

"Hey!" Hector hollered. "I'm lucid too! Do I get a sticker?"

The technician holding the jar stopped and looked at Hector's disembodied head and shook his own.

"Just put it in the case," said the lead technician, who seemed in charge.

"Damnedest thing I ever saw," the junior technician replied and set Hector's jar down inside a specialized carrying case. He closed it up and carried it away to the same biohazard hallway Hiram had disappeared into. A third technician picked up the wriggling burlap sack and set it down into its own sealed container.

The lead technician watched the last specimen disappear and then turned to the soldiers waiting at the back of the panel van.

"I'm drinking tonight. I don't care what the rules are," he said and then walked away.

CHAPTER 13

Dozens of technicians worked in a warehouse full of disembodied arms squirming on tables, held down by metal bars and zip ties. The technicians wore gloves as they used scalpels to cut through the skin of each arm. Once they exposed the bone, a small bone saw cut away part of the bone to reveal the marrow. They scraped out bits of marrow and placed them in test tubes, labeled with a code to match it to the specific arm band secured to the corresponding zombie forearm.

A second warehouse was a flurry of activity as armed guards removed and added walking zombies to a series of cages, so technicians could take DNA samples similar to the warehouse full of arms. But this warehouse was split into two sections, one devoted to ambulatory zombies and the other section to parts and pieces moving within sample jars and petri dishes. The primary job was just taking the DNA samples from bone marrow. Many of the technicians were medical and morgue technicians with experience identifying the MIA remains of service members from the various battlefields throughout the world. Despite their extensive field work, the proceedings in the last twenty-four hours had rattled more than a few of them. The dead shouldn't be squirming.

In three other labs on site, smaller squads of technicians worked in rooms full of centrifuges and other medical equipment, working meticulously to identify the DNA samples retrieved from each specimen. After several hours, a technician approached the lead scientist with a specific result. The scientist nodded his head as he looked over the paperwork. He sent the technician away and walked to one of the desk phones.

General Huckster sat in his pristine underground office. Various military photographs alongside framed medals and certificates adorned the walls. One wall held military journals, books of war, and tomes of scientific research. On his desk, next to his computer monitor, sat a solitary picture of a young blonde woman who smiled back at him. She wore a sundress and a necklace with a small quarter moon pendant made of the purest green jade. The general opened a folder and pulled a matching necklace from a small white envelope. He clenched the jewelry in his fist and closed his eyes. The phone suddenly rang. Wiping a tear from his eye, he picked the phone up and held it to his ear.

"Huckster," he said firmly. He listened for a moment, and the muscles in his jaw clenched tightly. He solemnly nodded his head.

"Thank you, Doctor Kane. I appreciate the heads up," he said and hung up the phone. He picked up the picture frame and swallowed hard. "Well, now we know for certain. Rest in peace, sweetheart."

He closed his eyes and the film reel in his head replayed the few memories he had with his daughter as she was growing up. They'd only spent a handful of birthdays, kindergarten and high school graduation and a few spring break vacations camping together. He mostly missed the day-to-day activities, as his wife Luna had been the one taking care of nearly every aspect of raising their only child. When Luna passed away from cancer, he'd done what he could to fill that gap in his daughter's life, but he was a poor substitute for her mother. There was a lot of tension at home, mostly because of his frequent absences for work; over the years, he spent more time deployed or away on a classified mission than he ever did at home. She'd finished the last two years of high school practically alone. He had wondered over the last few months if things would have been different if he'd just retired when Luna got sick. Now they were both gone and there was no way to make up for lost time.

He pushed himself away from the desk and stood up, fists clenched. He took a deep breath and made a grimace. With a sudden fury, he grabbed the computer keyboard and smashed it violently against the desk, knocking the computer monitor off the desk onto the floor. His executive assistant, Major Mead, came running to the door and opened it, looking in with concern. General Huckster looked up at him and dropped the remaining pieces of his keyboard onto the desk.

"Major, this, uh, keyboard appears to have malfunctioned. Get it replaced. Monitor too. But first, tell Lieutenant Iverson to secure Miss Riley in the access tunnel to Mister Simon's cell," General Huckster then held up his hand. "And leave her with her prosthetic limb free. That will give her a fighting chance."

"Yes sir," Major Mead replied and disappeared as quickly as he had come.

General Huckster looked around the office for a

moment and sighed. He grabbed his hat off a small hook on the wall by the door and left.

Martin stood by the sink in the futuristic plastic and metal cell he now called home. There was a complete and utter silence in the sealed chamber. As Martin scrubbed his shoe clean, he ruminated on the studies he'd read about absolute silence driving test subjects insane. He mused it wasn't effecting him because he had already lost his mind a long time ago. He found the absence of sound soothing. It calmed his mind more than anything else.

As he held up his shoe to inspect it, he noticed he'd missed a spot. He returned to scrubbing it clean.

Then he was back at the garage industrial sink in his childhood home, scrubbing his sneakers white while sounds of violence erupted from inside the home. Glass shattered and holes were punched in walls that had been patched dozens of times. Martin set the shoe down and wandered over to the door that led into the house. He peeked through the door, which was just slightly ajar. He saw nothing, but the shouts of anger from his stepfather were that much more pronounced.

Quietly, Martin snuck into the house and peered around the corner of the pantry into the kitchen. Just over the kitchen island, Martin watched as his stepfather swung his right arm at Martin's mother's face. Blood sprayed across the living room wall as it flew from her shattered face and she collapsed onto the ground.

"Get up, you stupid bitch!" Martin's stepfather yelled. He moved like he was kicking something on the ground.

Martin walked calmly into the kitchen and retrieved the cast-iron skillet from the morning's breakfast. It was still warm to the touch. He walked up behind his stepfather and swung the pan at his head. There was a loud crack as it struck the man's skull and he crumpled to the floor.

Martin went to his mother. "Mom, let's go," Martin whispered to her. She didn't move and her eyes were closed. Martin shook her and blinked.

"Mom," he repeated. Then he shouted, "*Mom!*"

He moved her head and her jaw hung limp, broken with the skin of her cheek torn. He set her head back as it was and checked for breathing. There was nothing he could detect. He felt for a pulse and found none.

Martin cried for a moment, tears running down his twelve-year-old face. Then, he shut his heart off from the world. His stepfather groaned behind him. Martin slipped his hand around the handle of the cast-iron skillet and tightened his grip.

He stood up and walked over to his stepfather, who was just opening his eyes. He raised his hand to the back of his head. Martin brought the skillet down on his face with a sickening crack. The stricken man wiggled for a moment before Martin brought the skillet down repeatedly. He didn't stop until the hated stepparent's head was a mash of bone, blood, and brain matter.

An electronic pop from the large television monitor to the left of him brought Martin out of his reverie. The fifty inch screen came to life. he glanced over to find the officer in command looking at him from the screen, which was positioned just above the toilet.

"Mister Simon, I trust you are enjoying your accommodations."

"Not exactly the Holiday Inn," Martin replied as he rinsed off his shoe and examined it.

"We believe it is more appropriate under the circumstances. That cell is actually impregnable. Safest place on this base. Nothing can get in and, well, nothing can get out."

Martin looked up into the mirror hanging over the sink. His face was a symphony of bruises and cuts from the beating he'd received in the interrogation room hours earlier. They'd never even asked him any questions. He absently ran his tongue over one of his broken teeth. Luckily, the break hadn't gone all the way through to the root. It was more of a chip. He mused the living had done more damage to him than the undead.

"My compliments to the engineer," Martin replied as returned his attention to drying off his shoe. He put it back on his foot. "Why am I in here again?"

"Well, we need you alive to conduct our experiments on the zombies. They have a peculiar homing instinct to you and only you. We placed them at several locations throughout the base."

"Alive? Must be why you stopped the 'interrogation' after only what, twenty minutes of intense 'questioning?'"

General Huckster grunted in response. "Only in the name of science were you kept alive," he responded. As he spoke, the picture on the screen changed to show several unique rooms in quick succession, each with zombies pushing forward in one particular direction in each room.

"We triangulated your position four hours before you arrived. Right about that time, I believe you had a zombie finger stuck in your rectum."

"I'll be happy not repeating that experience," Martin replied drily.

"Can you tell me how these victims of yours turned into zombies? We are very interested in that process," General Huckster asked as the screen brought his face back. Martin could see various monitors behind him, like the general was in some kind of control room.

"I don't know anything about it. I certainly didn't start it."

"We've matched the DNA to several of your known victims, but there are others that don't fit your profile."

"Profile?" Martin asked. "What profile?"

Martin knew exactly what the general was talking about, but wanted to know how much he knew and how much danger Martin and Bibi were in.

"Another pitiful profile assembled by the eggheads at the FBI," General Huckster responded. "Some kind of bullshit traumatic experience in your childhood drove you to commit crimes specifically targeting bullies. They assume removal of the right arm has something to do with the chief architect of your misery when you were having childhood difficulties." The words dripped from General Huckster's mouth with disdain.

"Difficulties?" Martin responded as he sat down on the single bed in the cell.

"I believe people are born evil and need to be eliminated with prejudice from society," the general replied. "Pansies who blame a rough childhood on the world and take it out on others are weak, pathetic criminals—cowardice of the highest order."

"I see," Martin said. "That's an interesting theory."

"Why did you decide to turn yourself in to us and not the police?"

"I didn't turn myself in. I needed protection. It seemed

you might have the resources to eliminate the threat."

"Oh, we rounded up all your undead assailants. Cost a pretty penny and a lot of red tape, but we've managed to clean up the mess you made."

"So, we can go then. Threat eliminated," Martin said as he stood up and faced the television.

General Huckster chuckled. "Let me show you something."

The screen changed to show a news clip showing Martin's warehouse surrounded by biohazard suited personnel.

"An FBI spokesman informed us the Handyman Killer was tracked to this warehouse and died in a prolonged firefight with agents," a woman's voice narrated the events surrounding the footage. "Right now, workers in biohazard suits are pulling body parts out of a large walk-in freezer that the Handyman Killer kept parts of his victims in. There are volatile chemicals at the site, and the FBI has enacted a one-mile evacuation area around the entire warehouse district. This is the last footage we got before authorities restricted the airspace around the area, citing public safety."

The picture cut off and General Huckster's face returned. "You're dead, Martin Simon. You're just not buried yet."

"I'm clearly not dead," Martin stated and held his arms out. General Huckster raised his eyebrows.

"We have several experiments you and your companions will be instrumental in helping us with."

"Why would I help you?" Martin asked.

General Huckster smiled. "Oh, you misunderstand. It doesn't require your cooperation."

"Then why are you talking to me at all?"

"I crave your pain," General Huckster replied. "It gives me joy."

"You can't hold us like this. We have rights," Martin replied. "Even suspected criminals have rights."

Huckster held up the paperwork Martin and Bibi signed earlier and smiled. "You and your girlfriend signed your lives away with this release of liability for injury, death or dismemberment in the course of government sanctioned experiments. Thank you. Makes my job so much easier." General Huckster dropped his smile and continued. "Dead or alive, we own you."

The television picture went black. Martin sat down and held his head between his hands. He looked at the sink. He got up and washed his hands.

CHAPTER 14

Bibi backed up into the cell they trapped her in. Two men lay unconscious on the floor and three more crowded the doorway. They moved inside slowly and the last one had a stick with a metallic tip he held out towards Bibi. Behind them, additional personnel dragged the unconscious men out of the cell.

"We don't want to hurt you," the man with the stick said.

"Really?" Bibi replied. "You wanna fuck me then? I'll rip your tiny dicks off!"

They rushed her all at once. The man with the stick hit her with the cattle prod and sent a jolt of electricity into her. She screamed. Momentarily distracted by the pain, the men corralled her and dragged her out. She kicked at them, but they avoided the worst of her wrath. Once they got her out of the cell, a medical technician jabbed a syringe into her neck.

After a few minutes, the fight seemed to go out of her and she slumped in their arms.

"Quickly, now," the tech shouted. "It's only good for about fifteen minutes."

The men carried her limp body away. The technician

watched them go. When the double doors shut behind them as they entered another tunnel, the tech looked at the syringe and threw it into a corner, shattering it.

"This is bullshit," he muttered and walked away in the other direction.

General Huckster sat at his computer as Major Mead walked in.

"General, sir," the executive assistant said as he saluted. The general saluted back without getting up.

"Major Mead, what do you have to report?" General Huckster said as he continued looking at the monitor.

"Miss Riley has been placed in the tunnel, per your request. She injured several personnel during the move. The doctor thinks two men may have suffered concussions."

"She's got a lot of fight in her," General Huckster said as he nodded.

"Sir, permission to speak freely?" Major Mead asked. General Huckster sighed and nodded. He looked up at his exec.

"This isn't exactly ethical, sir," Major Mead stated. "The young lady, in particular, hasn't done anything to deserve this type of treatment."

"Your concern has been duly noted, Major," General Huckster replied as he looked back at the monitor.

"You can still carry on without injury to her," Major Mead replied.

"That's enough, Major!" General Huckster shouted as he stood up. "This is my decision, and if you have a problem with it, I will relieve you of duty and you'll be scrubbing toilets in Botswana. Do I make myself clear?"

"Yes sir," Major Mead replied. "Sorry, sir."

"Get the technicians assembled. We'll get this done now before any other bleeding hearts decide they need a court martial!" General Huckster demanded.

Major Mead saluted and left the room.

Minutes later, the exec returned and saluted again. The general stood up and returned the salute.

"I have notified the technicians to report to their duty stations," Major Mead replied.

"Excellent," General Huckster said as he stepped around the desk. "Now pack your things and go home."

"Sir?" Major Mead stepped backward in shock.

"You're done here, Jay. Go home. You're relieved of duty. You'll get new orders in a week. Now get off my base," General Huckster said calmly and walked by the stunned junior officer.

Martin scrubbed one of the thick plastic windows, trying to remove a greasy smear. He suspected it was some type of lubricant for the machinery that moved the mobile walls of his cell. The substance proved difficult to eliminate with the simplistic cleaning supplies in the cell. He wished for a little citrus just to cut the oily base of the stain. The view screen popped on behind him.

"Glad to see you're keeping busy, Mister Simon," General Huckster said.

"Please call me Martin," he replied as he licked his swelled lower lip, a product of the beating he'd suffered earlier. "We're on such friendly terms, I feel strange not addressing each other by our first name."

"Gallows humor, delightful," the officer replied. "We

have some advanced DNA testing results here I thought I would share."

Martin stopped cleaning the window and sat down on the bunk. "Whatever you say, General...?" Martin said as he raised his eyebrows.

"You'll learn my name in good time. Don't worry. Let me tell you about your car first," General Huckster said. "We pulled your car apart, examining each piece and testing various fluids and bits of DNA. They tell me some of the body fluids can't provide reliable DNA–it breaks down when exposed to the elements like the hot sun."

"Thanks for the science class lecture," Martin quipped. "Maybe just slide the cliff notes under the cell door instead."

General Huckster cleared his throat and pressed on. "There were bits on bone and other materials–we removed a skull from one of your front headlights."

"Car wash didn't get it out, and I didn't have time to play skull mechanic."

"Of course you didn't," General Huckster acknowledged testily. "We matched the DNA from one of those bits to one of the arms you so generously preserved for the authorities in your walk-in freezer."

"We all need our trophies," Martin replied.

"One of those trophies and the DNA strewn across the radiator of your vehicle matched one Rebecca Huckster," the general said and his voice rose with the name he announced.

Martin looked up at the television and shrugged his shoulders. "She was an animal abuser and deserved what she got," Martin replied. "What of it?"

"I'm General Huckster. Rebecca was my daughter. My

only child."

"Well," Martin replied. "Shit."

"Shit, indeed," General Huckster replied through gritted teeth. "I have a treat for you, murderer. You destroyed someone I care about, so I thought I would return the favor."

On the screen, a picture of Bibi shackled in a hallway appeared. They secured her feet in leg irons chained to the floor and her left arm above her head via a wrist cuff welded to a chain secured to an eye bolt in the ceiling. Her right prosthetic arm was free, but there was no way she could reach any of the shackles to free herself.

Martin jumped up and approached the screen. "Let her go!" Martin shouted. "She didn't hurt anybody!"

"Well, then, she'll match the rest of your victims, won't she?"

Bibi looked at the camera when she heard Huckster's voice coming from it. "When I get outta here, I'm cutting off your fucking head!" she shouted.

"Charming to the last," General Huckster mused, and then cleared his throat. "The experiment we are testing today is a zombie obstacle course. In the past, Martin's zombies have hurt no one who got out of their way. Today, we see what happens when someone comes between them and their target... and they can't get out of the way."

A wall came down outside Martin's cell opposite the television screen, revealing Bibi's back visible in the tunnel. He pounded on the window.

"Bibi!" Martin shouted. Bibi looked over her shoulder and caught the barest glimpse of Martin trapped behind a thick wall of plastic and bulletproof glass.

"And now, for the guests of honor. Let's see if the

zombies are hungry today," General Huckster announced calmly.

An immense wall at the entrance to the tunnel slowly dropped and revealed hundreds of zombies to Bibi's widening eyes. They immediately stumbled forward, climbing over the wall before it had completely dropped into the floor. The undead pressed inexorably forward as Bibi's face went pale. Before the first one reached her, though, she put on her battle face.

"When I'm done with these bozos, I'm coming for you, asshole," she whispered.

As the zombies pressed forward, condensing in the single tunnel, the first of them merely went around Bibi. As they crowded the tunnel, they tried to go through Bibi. She fought them off as valiantly as she could, head butting a few and knocking a few of them back with her prosthetic arm.

"Leave her alone! She's innocent!" Martin shouted again.

Finally, the sheer weight and mass of the zombies coming through the tunnel overwhelmed Bibi. The zombies bit and scratched her as they came through, sending little rivulets of blood down her body. Finally, they ripped her left hand out of the shackle and the feisty blonde went down under the press of zombies. The zombies surged forward, crushing her under their weight. She screamed for a few moments and then went silent.

"Nooo!" Martin screamed as he beat his hands on the window. His eyes focused on the area Bibi had disappeared. He barely noticed the flood of zombies surrounding his impregnable cell.

From the slightly elevated cell floor, Martin could see

over the approaching zombies. When the last of the zombies left the tunnel, he saw Bibi's lifeless body lying on the floor. Hiram wandered into the tunnel from the space beyond and stopped at Bibi's feet. The undead serial killer shook his head.

"What a shame. She had real fire," Hiram said. He looked up and saw Martin with tears in his eyes. "A debt paid, but not as I had wished."

Martin glanced at Hiram and sighed. He didn't blame Hiram for Bibi's death. He'd merely wanted to kill Martin. Bibi had volunteered to come along for the ride. No, the real villain in Martin's eyes was Huckster. Martin turned to the video screen.

"You better kill me," Martin said calmly. "Because if you don't, I will put you on a spit and roast you alive like a pig."

The zombies surrounding his cell banged on the walls, trying to find a way in to their prey.

"I'll cut off your toes while you're still alive and shove them down your throat. While I strip the skin off your body, I'll chuckle as you're turning over that fiery pit, begging for mercy. I'll keep slicing off pieces of your flesh until I see your eyes roll into the back of your head, and then I'll beat your head to a pulp until your battered skull drops off your neck."

General Huckster shrugged. "You took from me and I took from you," he replied. "Your threats mean little to me. I enjoy watching you suffer."

"You took an innocent life, while I took a pathetic bully who learned her evil ways from you. How does it feel knowing you were such a failure as a father that you doomed your only daughter to die a premature death?"

General Huckster snarled at Martin. "I will guarantee you can never kill again!" he shouted.

There was an audible click and a whirr in Martin's cell. A hiss of escaping pressure preceded the ceiling of the cell rising.

"General, no! We haven't finished the experiments!" A voice off the camera yelled at Huckster.

"This project is done when I say it's done!" General Huckster shouted to someone out of view.

As the walls of the cell lowered, the zombies' attempts to get at Martin became more frenzied.

Huckster switched to a different camera view showing the exterior of the cell. Sparks flew as the television screen inside the cell collided with the toilet below and it tore from the lowering wall, falling to the floor of the cell with a loud clatter.

Martin made eye contact with Hiram and nodded. Hiram nodded back. "So long, old friend," Hiram said.

Martin gave out a battle cry as the zombies tumbled over the wall and scrambled toward him. He kicked, punched and did everything in his power to defend himself, but he went down under the avalanche of zombies in just seconds. A few minutes later, the squirming mass of zombies stopped moving entirely. The spell giving them animation faded.

"Now, I can die in peace," Hiram said as he looked down at his body and his shoulders slumped. "Crap, I'm already dead."

All the remaining zombies that could not reach Martin sat down where they were, their mission complete, and lost the spectral energy that kept them animated. Hiram walked over to the pile of zombies and watched them lose their grasp on their undead existence. As he watched the last one fall silent, he held his hand up in front of his face and waved it slowly.

"Why am I still moving?" he wondered aloud. He turned around, looked at Bibi's fallen form and raised an eyebrow.

CHAPTER 15

A young soldier carried a duffel bag into General Huckster's office and saluted. The general frowned at him as he saluted back.

"Sergeant, are you lost?" General Huckster asked.

The soldier shook his head and held up the bag. "Sir, I have the young lady's belongings and I had a question."

"Dispose of them in the incinerator as per standard protocol. Is that all? I think I'll have a word with your supervisor," General Huckster looked back at his computer screen.

"But, sir, there's a really wicked machete in there. I could sell it online and—"

"Sergeant, don't force me to make you the subject of one of our experiments. Dismissed."

The sergeant saluted and exited the room. There was a slight commotion in the hallway before the sergeant stumbled back into the office with a bloody gash across his face, blood spurting from a gash in his neck. His eyes rolled back in his head and he fell to the ground. Bibi walked around the corner with a machete in her bloodied left hand. Huckster whipped open a drawer and reached for his gun. Bibi threw the machete, hitting him in the right shoulder, preventing him from using his right arm. He slammed his left fist down on a big red button on the desk. Alarms went off and a metal barrier slid down in front of the office door, sealing the office shut, with Bibi and General Huckster inside.

Before he could grab his gun with his left hand, Bibi jumped over the desk with a scream and tackled him to the floor.

"Warning, containment breach. Facility is in lockdown. All personnel report to your stations," the overhead speaker announced.

Bibi pulled the machete out of Huckster's shoulder. The general grimaced in pain as he reached for Bibi with his left hand. Bibi whipped the machete through his left wrist like a hot knife through butter. General Huckster screamed out. Bibi used both hands to grab the machete and plunged it between her legs into his abdomen. Blood gushed up into the air for a moment before she climbed off him. Blood continued to pour out of the wound and he wheezed in pain.

"Told you I was going to cut your fucking head off," Bibi said as she pulled the machete out of his belly. She hacked away at the general's neck, spraying blood everywhere. Minutes passed and finally Bibi stopped swinging the blade. She picked up the general's head by the hair like a trophy and screamed in triumph.

"Just keep wrapping up the bodies until we get the all clear," one of the personnel in HazMat suits said as he watched the other suited personnel loading zombie bodies and parts into body bags. There were hundreds of zombies and they'd only just made a dent in the pile.

Two personnel held guns on Hiram as he stood against a wall facing them.

"Think you guys could put me in the incinerator with the bodies so I can leave this mortal coil?" Hiram asked them.

"You're needed for further experiments," one of the armed men replied.

"*Maravilloso*," Hiram said.

The overhead speakers sprang to life.

"Lockdown ended. Resume normal operations."

"Boss," one tech loading bodies said. "We need more body bags."

"Okay," the supervisor replied. "Everyone wrap it up. We have to stop until supply can send us some more. All personnel clear the room for the night."

The ten personnel, including the armed ones, cleared the room, marching Hiram out ahead of them. They turned the lights off and only the red emergency lights by the doors illuminated the pile of dead bodies in the center of the room.

The soldiers marched Hiram to another building. As they walked him in, Hiram recognized some of the equipment in the room. "You sure the morgue is the right place for me?" he asked one of the armed men.

The man pointed his gun at a large cage in the far corner of the room with an unlocked door. "Your new home away from home, uh, dead dude," the soldier said.

"Undead," Hiram replied as he walked to the cage and entered it. The soldier secured the door and lowered his weapon.

"You're a strange and unholy fuck," the soldier stated and turned his back on Hiram as he walked away. On one shelf along the wall, Hector yelled "Boo" from inside his jar and the soldier jumped, accidentally firing a round into the ceiling.

"Shit, Collins!" another technician yelled as he entered the room. "Keep your shit together, man!"

"I hate these unholy fucks," Collins replied.

"Yeah, we got that the first time," Hiram said.

Collins looked back at Hiram and shook his head. The other technician clapped Collins on the shoulder.

"We need to get you laid, Collins. Relieve some of that tension. I know just the girl for you. Works at the Double D."

The two men exited the room. The room was quiet for a moment.

"Those honkies got some issues, eh?" Hector called out.

"Indeed they do," Hiram replied. He looked around his cage and saw a bucket, presumably for waste use. He turned it over, sat down on it, and checked out Hector's jar on the shelf across the room. There wasn't much in the way of movement, just occasional moments of inane chatter from the undead gang member. Hiram sighed.

"And I thought the room full of zombies was boring."

The sealed door to General Huckster's office opened and three armed soldiers in HazMat suits entered the room. They fanned out in the small room.

"Oh shit!" one of them said as their foot kicked General Huckster's head. It rolled and hit the wall.

Another of the soldiers looked at Bibi lying on her back on the floor, dead eyes staring at the ceiling. She was just as motionless and covered in blood as General Huckster's beheaded body behind the desk. The soldiers looked all around the room, searching under the desk and even on the shelves.

"All clear," one soldier announced.

Lab technicians in HazMat suits entered the room and examined the bodies. "Let's move them to the morgue for a proper post mortem," the lead technician said. "Whatever killed them isn't in here anymore. Use the last of the body bags and remove them. Contact the clean-up crew and notify Major Mead."

"I heard Major Mead was relieved," one of the other technicians replied.

"Did you hear who replaced him?" The lead technician asked.

"No."

"Then notify Major Mead," the lead technician said. "This chain of command is already fucked up enough as it is."

"Ain't that the truth," the second technician replied as he left the room. The remaining personnel loaded bodies and scooped up body parts into the body bags.

Hiram watched as the suited technicians carried the three body bags from General Huckster's office past him to the storage drawers in the wall. They placed one in each of them and closed the refrigerated cubicles.

The sunlight streaming in through the doors of the morgue grew fainter as night approached and the temperature outside dropped. The soldiers finished up their paperwork quickly and left the morgue area. All was quiet.

Inside one of the morgue drawers, Hiram heard movement. The door popped open and Bibi's arm dropped outside the edge of the opening as she pulled herself out, still partially enclosed in the body bag. After she plopped onto the floor, she unzipped the bag the rest of the way and climbed out stiffly. She reached inside her jeans and retrieved her machete.

The sound of approaching footsteps drew her attention to the front door. She ran next to the door and hid next to one of the large metal cabinets. A HazMat suited technician entered the room and walked toward Hiram.

Bibi snuck up behind him and bit him in the shoulder, piercing the HazMat suit and his skin. He screamed and twisted out of her grasp. Bibi shoved the machete into his back through his heart. He fell to the floor as a pool of blood spread out on the linoleum floor beneath him. Bibi licked the machete blade and then her lips. Her eyes landed on Hiram. She walked over to the cage and Hiram stood up as she approached.

"Bibi," Hiram said. "I'm truly sorry you have to endure this undead nightmare."

"Do you know where Martin is?" Bibi asked.

Hiram nodded. "What I wished for came to pass. While I feel closure, seeing him ripped to pieces gave me no joy or satisfaction. It was a hollow victory, after all."

Bibi stumbled backward for a moment. "He's dead?"

Hiram sat down as the enormity of spending eternity locked up and experimented on weighed on him. Still, he had to fill Bibi in even as he contemplated his own cursed existence.

"Probably the only genuine emotion he ever showed in his life was when you died. He even hastened his own death to satisfy my last wish. He was honorable to the last. Now, I guess I just wait for them to finish me off."

Bibi shook her head and grinned. "I got a better idea."

She bent down over the dead technician and rummaged through his pockets. She located a key and walked back to Hiram's cage door. The key fit the lock. She unlocked the cell door and opened it. Hiram stepped out and looked around.

"What now?" Hiram asked.

On the floor, the dead lab technician stirred and rose. They watched as he stood up, looked at them both with glazed over eyes and then walked out the door of the morgue.

"Let's get this undead party started," Bibi said. She looked at Hiram with a wicked grin, which he returned.

"I believe Pandora's Box has been opened," Hiram said with a nod.

Bibi and Hiram walked out into the cool evening air. They caught a passing security guard by surprise. Their combined attack quickly overwhelmed him. Behind the fallen guard, heat rose from the hood of an SUV parked by the building. Bibi searched the dead body for keys and came up lucky again. She climbed into the driver's seat as Hiram took shotgun position next to her.

Another soldier ran up toward the front of their car. The undead lab technician was close behind him. The soldier fired his gun at the technician as he ran by the SUV. Bibi opened the driver's side door and knocked the soldier to the ground. The lab technician zombie was on him in seconds. The soldier screamed as the zombie bit into his face.

"I believe I have developed contempt for the living," Bibi said.

"Better late than never," Hiram replied.

She turned from the zombie feeding frenzy outside her car door and looked at Hiram.

"I'm going to go see some old friends. You game?" she asked him.

"I think I'm going to like this undead life," Hiram said and smiled.

Bibi closed the door and they drove around the feeding zombie. Another soldier happened by and Hiram knocked him to the ground with his own door. The zombified lab technician heard the commotion and immediately attacked the fresh, vulnerable target.

Bibi and Hiram drove off into the dark desert night.

Hector's head, still in the jar on a shelf, stared at the door.

"I can't believe they left me behind," Hector said. On the other side of the morgue, a large freezer door opened and a headless body pushed its way out. The body started feeling around the walls in the dark.

"Hey, over here!"

The headless body knocked over several things in its search, including the jar Hector's head was in, which shattered when it hit the floor. Hector bit the pant leg. The hands reached down, found the head, and then placed it on the neck.

"All right!" Hector shouted. He walked forward and his head began to fall off. He quickly grabbed it.

"Aww, man! That ain't cool!" Hector whined. He looked through the morgue equipment and found a surgical stapler. After stapling his neck all the way around to keep his head on, he turned on the lights, and went to the mirror hung above an industrial sink to examine his handiwork.

"*Chicas* love piercings and scars! This is gonna be great!"

Hector walked out of the morgue into the dark night that echoed with the screams of frightened victims all over the base.

Steam rose into the cool desert air from the pile of dead bodies stacked in the middle of the defunct cell. Random bursts of gunfire followed by blood curdling shouts punctuated the calm silence in the room as the zombie infestation spread throughout the base.

The dead body at the top of the pile wiggled slightly. Several of the bodies at the pinnacle of the fleshy pyramid shook as if something erupted from below them.

From the center of the pile, a single bloody and shredded arm shot upward. It grabbed the bodies on top and roughly pushed them aside. Muted grunts and curses sounded from deep below the pile of corpses. After several minutes of shoving bodies and squirming upward, Martin emerged from the dog pile of corpses. He looked around at the room. In the red of the emergency lights, the various wounds and shredded nature of his flesh became apparent. Torn flesh from bite marks covered one side of his face, and a portion of his bloody scalp dangled precariously from the back of his skull. His right eye was swollen shut, while his left eye was a grey, creamy version of its former self. His skin took on a pale pallor where it wasn't missing. Several bloody wounds dotted his torso where chunks of flesh exhibited various stages of being torn off his body.

He blinked and looked down at his damaged body.

"Aww, shit," he said and two teeth flew out of his mouth. After he frowned at the freshly liberated teeth, he shook his head to clear the cobwebs. With a quick glance to where Bibi had been, Martin growled and redoubled his efforts to extricate himself from the thousands of pounds of dead bodies holding him down.

"She's in the same boat," he grunted as he pulled himself out of the pile, revealing more damage to his body. He climbed off the pile and stumbled across the floor. He looked down and noticed his left foot was bare and part of it was missing.

"Dammit," he cursed and turned back to the steaming pile of bodies. Digging through the the cadavers, he found a gangly left leg with an old decrepit left shoe still on the foot. Pulling at the shoe, he removed the entire foot from the leg. He sighed as he dug the former owner's remains out of the shoe before putting the shoe on and walking out, shaking his head. "What a world."

As Martin shuffled along, he limped on the left leg. The partial missing foot gave him balance problems. "I always thought the shuffling thing was cliché. Now I get it."

Two soldiers ran by him, terrified. Martin calmly watched them pass. On their heels, two zombie soldiers ran/shambled along after their prey. They paused briefly to look at him in confusion. Martin observed them in wonder.

A shot rang out and a piece of one of the zombies in front of Martin flew off, refocusing the undead pair's attention on the soldiers they pursued. They resumed their chase after the live soldiers.

Martin looked in the direction the soldiers had come from and observed several buildings on fire. Brief staccatos of gun fire, shouts, screams and general mayhem punctuated the undead chaos on the base. Martin turned and walked the other way.

Near the outskirts of the base buildings, Martin came upon an SUV partially embedded in the side of a small hangar. Inside the SUV, two zombies fed on a body behind the wheel. Martin pulled the door open and pulled the body out onto the ground. The zombies inside scrambled out of the car after the meal, ignoring Martin entirely.

Martin climbed into the SUV. The keys were still in the ignition. He started up the SUV and backed out of the building, which collapsed a bit more upon the vehicle being removed. The zombies on the ground didn't take notice of it. Martin drove away.

CHAPTER 16

The lights of the Double D strip club shone into the desert night, far away from the lights of the Vegas strip. Some lights in the sign had burned out years ago, including the "o" in "Double." The parking lot had only a few trucks in it. It was a slow night at this gentlemen's club from days gone by.

Bibi and Hiram pulled up in the mostly empty parking lot of the dingy little building. Bibi stepped out onto an asphalt surface so broken it was nearly gravel and looked southwest at the lights of the strip shining in the distance.

"I lived a short way from here," Bibi remarked as she gazed west. Hiram came up next to her, standing taller than he had when they'd first met. He seemed to have almost come back to life. "I used to fantasize there was a better life just over there where the lights touched the sky."

"Well, from what I understand, it was better than what you left behind here."

"It really didn't get noticeably better even when I left the hell that was home. It wasn't until Martin... and now he's gone."

Bibi cleared her throat and turned around to face the

faded red paint on the building in front of them.

"Looks like they didn't bother with any upkeep after I left," she remarked as she stepped forward.

"Pretty sure the clientele that frequents this place doesn't mind," Hiram said.

When they got halfway across the parking lot, the doors suddenly pushed open and a middle-aged man came flying out, hitting the ground and rolling to a stop. He pushed himself to his feet and staggered toward a truck in the parking lot.

"We may face some resistance entering," Hiram remarked.

"Oh, I don't think that will be a problem," Bibi said as she pulled open the red door. A large, stocky black man approached them from the inner set of double doors. He held up his hand and shook his head.

"It ain't fuckin' Halloween," he said in a deep raspy voice. "I don't care how cheap this club is, you ain't coming in here looking like shit."

Bibi turned to Hiram and winked, then slid her machete out from under her jacket and swung the blade into the doorman's crotch. The shocked man doubled over, screaming as blood burst forth from a severed femoral artery. Bibi grabbed his collar and pulled his ear close to her.

"Yes, we are," she whispered in his ear. Then she bit off his ear, eliciting even higher, fresh screams from the man. She pushed him over and he lay writhing on the ground.

The woman at the walk-up window dropped out of sight with a slightly muttered, "Oh shit!" Bibi glanced at the window before she wiped her machete off on the doorman's back. She knew from experience that there wasn't a phone in the booth, but the employee might have her cell on her even though they were prohibited on premises.

Another young woman dressed in a very skimpy outfit appeared at the inner doors, saw the doorman on the ground in a pool of blood and screamed at the sight of Bibi walking toward her wielding a machete streaked with crimson. She ran back into the building.

"Call nine-one-one!" She hollered as she ran for the dressing rooms.

Bibi and Hiram followed her into the building.

Half a dozen patrons lined the three raised platforms as girls on stage danced topless to the music piping through the sound system. The men stopped watching the girls to glance at the greeter as she ran by screaming. As they looked toward the front door, the dancers stopped to see what they were looking at. They all saw Bibi and Hiram. Panic ensued.

Bibi grinned at Hiram. "Have fun, Hiram. I need a drink," Bibi said to him as she turned right and continued to walk toward the bar.

"Don't mind if I do," Hiram replied and ran at the patrons, taking turns attacking them. Some men tried to defend the dancers, but most lost their nerve when the blows that hit Hiram did nothing and they wound up getting bitten, scratched or pummeled by him. He eventually ran after the dancers, who retreated and barricaded themselves in the dressing room.

Bibi walked straight to the bar, her path unwavering. An old woman behind the bar, dressed in a white shirt indicative of a bartender, watched her approach impassively. She was a tough old broad with leathery skin and a no shit attitude.

"Well," the old woman said as she set the glass she was drying down on the counter. "Look what the garbage man dragged in. What the fuck are you doin' here?"

"Just came to pay my respects, Ma," Bibi said with a smile.

Phyllis snorted. "Respects, my ass. You look like shit."

Phyllis turned to look at Hiram engaging in full-blown carnage around the rest of the bar and shook her head. She returned her attention to Bibi.

"You and your boyfriend on drugs? I don't need that shit in here, ya little bitch!"

"Always the loving mother. So sharing," Bibi replied with a grim smile.

"Fuck you—you liked the sex as much as they did," Phyllis replied. She grabbed a bottle of whiskey and poured a shot down her throat.

"Is that how you keep from going crazy? Keep telling yourself your daughter enjoyed getting raped by all your lovers?"

"Go to hell."

Bibi jumped onto the bar and crouched down, leaning into Phyllis' face. "I'm already there—I came to share!"

Phyllis cocked the shotgun she was holding out of sight under the bar. Bibi looked down at the weapon.

"Aw, shit," Bibi murmured just before the shotgun went off. As Bibi flew backward, chunks of her undead abdomen flew into the air. Phyllis' face and torso got a generous spray of dark red fluid from Bibi's fresh wound.

Bibi lay on the floor, clutching her stomach. The old woman cackled as she cocked the weapon again and came out from behind the bar. She approached her daughter on the ground. She stepped next to her and lowered the shotgun to Bibi's head.

"You shoulda stayed away, you stupid whore," the old woman said.

In a flash, Bibi deflected the shotgun as it went off, blowing a hole through the back of an upholstered booth. Bibi bit deeply into her mother's leg. Phyllis screamed and jerked her leg out of Bibi's mouth. She back pedaled before bumping into the bar.

Bibi jumped up and grabbed her machete from the floor. She swung it at Phyllis, who blocked the attack with the shotgun. They battled through the club, getting in blows on each other as Hiram busied himself tearing apart the rest of the club, patrons and dancers in the background.

Phyllis finally got the best of Bibi and knocked her down. The old woman raised the gun above her head, intending to use it as a club. Bibi did a fancy martial arts move and wound up standing next to her mother. Bibi sliced her opponent's hands off at the wrist. Phyllis screamed as her hands and the shotgun fell to the floor. Blood spurted from the ends of her forearms.

Bibi stepped back up and admired her handiwork. "Hands off. Just like I told you to tell your fucking boyfriends," Bibi sneered as she jammed the machete into the Phyllis' mouth until it poked out the back of her head, silencing her screams. The dead woman slid off the machete and fell to the floor.

Bibi turned around and saw Hiram standing there watching her. All around him, people were dead or moaning and crawling along the floor, injured and bleeding.

"So, are we done here?" he asked.

"Yeah. Just came to say goodbye to mom," Bibi said as she kicked her mother's dead head. Hiram smiled, and they walked out through the double doors.

"Just two of them. Please hurry!" the young woman's voice whispered out of sight.

"I think we've overstayed our welcome," Hiram smirked.

The motionless doorman lay on the floor on his back, his waxy dead eyes fixed on the pale stucco tiles in the ceiling. They walked by him as though he was just a misplaced piece of furniture, stepping over his legs that blocked the outer exit doors.

"I'll navigate," Bibi said as she pointed at the driver's side of the SUV. "I know the area."

Hiram adjusted his trajectory. Sirens in the distance announced the approach of the police. The duo quickly got into the car and pulled out of the parking lot. They drove down a side street away from the approaching authorities.

Inside the club, a man and a dancer stood up inside the DJ booth. The man zipped up his pants as the topless dancer licked her lips, wiped something off her chin, and then licked off her fingers. Reaching for the DJ controls, the man stopped as he looked at the carnage around the club.

"Oh, this blows," the dancer whispered just before the zombie doorman stumbled in through the double doors and locked his eyes on them. He grinned, and they screamed.

On a bedside table in a dark bedroom, the phone rang. An older man sat up and reached for it. He fumbled it slightly before bringing it to his ear. He ran his free hand over his bald head as he took a deep breath.

"Brooks here," he said. He listened for a moment and grimaced.

"All right. Break out the codebook—we are officially at base threat level Z3. Follow the instructions in the book. Hell, the ink's probably still wet," Brooks said into the phone. He hung up the phone and vigorously rubbed his face as he drew in another deep breath.

He looked over at his sleeping wife and touched her arm gently, caressing it lightly. She stirred.

"Got to go to work, babe," he whispered softly. She mumbled something and went back to sleep. Brooks got up and hurried to his closet.

Fighter jets flew over the base as they let bombs drop on targets down below, lighting up the night sky with an orange hue. Napalm came to visit Area 51. Humans and zombies alike burned down below as the volatile substance enveloped them with all-encompassing flames.

Brooks watched the burning base from a helicopter and shook his head. Behind him, Captain Rivas, a young officer with dark hair and a stern jaw, leaned forward and tapped his shoulder.

"What is it, Captain?" General Brooks asked.

"Sir, there are reports of an infection site at the Double D."

Brooks shook his head. "That damn Huckster," he grumbled. "I loved that club."

He turned to Captain Rivas. "Send Alpha team to the new infection site. Inform Command Post to continue to monitor the police bands and listen for anything unusual. This isn't over yet."

The helicopter flew over the rest of the base, lit up by fire all around. It was accompanied by additional helicopters equipped with searchlights that scoured the land around the base for any signs of movement. Two of the helicopters peeled off toward the south in the direction of the Double D.

CHAPTER 17

Bibi watched the lights of the Vegas Strip go by as they sped along the highway. She looked over at Hiram.

"We're not stopping here?" she asked.

"Not unless you have another personal grudge to satisfy," Hiram said as he shook his head. "Sin City is already damned. They don't need any help from us."

They both laughed. Bibi looked again at the lights as they whizzed by.

"Hiram, why are we still alive or whatever this is?" Bibi asked.

"Well, I've had quite a bit of time to ponder this. I can only assume its vengeance that drives us, but how we're still animated after death, it gets fuzzier. Perhaps post spell zombies won't drop when the spell ends. I was at or near the flash point of the spell going off, so I seem to be a special case in that matter."

"I still have some debts to pay, so I'll be around for a while," Bibi said.

"As do I, dear girl," Hiram agreed. "Next stop, the city of angels."

Martin slowed down on the highway as he drove by the Double D Nightclub, visible from the road. He pulled off to the side so he could get a better view. Other cars had stopped as well.

Police surrounded the building and actively fired at zombies coming from inside the building. The zombies weren't the least bit affected by the gunfire. Two of them reached a cop closest to the club and tore into him. The other police shouted an order to retreat.

"Happy Mother's Day, Phyllis," Martin murmured. He looked around the parking lot and didn't see any military vehicles. "So, they stopped by but didn't stay. Not sure where Hiram would go, but Bibi…"

Martin climbed back in the car and continued his drive through Vegas on his way to Los Angeles. He passed the same lights on the Strip, but they faded a bit as the sun rose in the East.

As the sun rose behind them, Hiram peered down at the gas gauge. It was near empty.

"Well, this should be interesting," he said. "We need gas. These government vehicles suck on efficiency."

"I can't say Martin's car was much better," Bibi replied. She pointed at the gas station they stopped at before where she'd bought the air fresheners she stuck on Hiram. "Who knew we'd be a repeat customer?"

"You have a card or something?" Hiram asked as he pulled up to the pump.

"No," Bibi said. "I didn't think to grab my stuff they took from me. I guess I didn't plan very well."

"Not to worry, we probably shouldn't be using a card, anyway. Much easier to track us that way. I'll handle it inside. Just wait for my signal and start pumping," Hiram said.

Bibi nodded.

Hiram got out and walked to the convenience store part of the station.

Bibi watched the door for a few minutes and then a police car pulled in to the parking lot far away from them and stopped. Bibi kept looking back and forth between the cop and the store. Finally, Hiram appeared and gave her a thumbs-up. Bibi got out and started pumping gas as Hiram walked calmly back to the car.

Bibi pumped the gas and kept glancing at the police car. The police officer inside seemed to only pay attention to his phone as he stared straight ahead, not even casually glancing their way.

Inside the police car, Officer Dan Billings chatted on his cell phone. "Honey, I swear–right, sorry, I'll stop calling you honey. She came on to me," he said and ran his fingers through his hair. "She meant nothing to me. You're the only one for me! Right, I mean, there was just the one time…"

Bibi finished pumping the gas and sighed with relief.

"Let's go," she said. Hiram nodded and climbed into the driver's seat. Bibi climbed in and they pulled back out onto the highway.

Dan got out of the car and continued his conversation.

"You know you mean everything to me," he continued. "That's why I realized it was a mistake to throw everything we have away on a one-night stand!... What? Well, you can't listen to what she says. She's not very trustworthy, so... Hello? Hello?!"

He tucked the phone in his pocket.

"Fuck!" he shouted and walked to the convenience store. Continuing inside, he grabbed a package of donuts, stopped at the coffee bar, and filled a cup. As he put a lid on, he heard a groan. Looking around carefully, he didn't see anyone, but noticed the clerk wasn't at the counter.

"Hello?" he shouted as he walked up to the counter. "Could I get some service, please? I need to get back on the road."

A single bloody hand grabbed the counter, and the clerk pulled himself up. "Jesus!" Dan screamed and stepped back. "Are you all right?"

The clerk growled at him and jumped up on the counter. Dan ran for the door, but the clerk zombie fell onto his back and chewed on the officer's shoulder. Dan screamed and fumbled for his weapon. The zombie took a chunk out of Dan's neck before he could get his gun out of the holster.

Dan put the gun against the attacker's forehead and fired. Gray matter and blood sprayed all over Dan and the floor as the zombie collapsed and stopped moving. Dan crawled out from under the zombie, leaving his own blood trail behind on the floor. Blood gushed from his neck wound. Dan pushed himself into a seated position, leaning his back against the walk-in cooler. He grabbed at the neck wound as he tried to stop the bleeding, but the blood loss was so severe he passed out within a few minutes.

Shelly sat on a desk while Javier, a young Mexican maintenance man, fucked her rapidly. She moaned as she grabbed his shoulders. Javier tensed up as he reached orgasm. Shelly looked disgusted.

"Is that it?" she asked.

Javier shrugged his shoulders as he stepped back, dropped the rubber in a trash can, and zipped up his jeans. Shelly dropped off the counter and rearranged her skirt and underwear.

"So, I'll call you later?" Javier asked, as he ran a comb through his hair.

"Oh, sure," Shelly sneered. "When you can fuck for longer than five minutes. Which is probably never."

Javier turned around and walked to the door. "Whatever, *puta*," Javier said, as he walked out. Shelly caught the door as he walked away from the building.

"I need a bull, Javier!" she shouted. "Not a Chihuahua!"

Javier flipped her the bird as he picked up his leaf blower and disappeared into the complex. Shelly straightened her hair and looked at the calendar for the day. There were no appointments.

"Fuck this. I need to get laid for real."

She grabbed her keys and walked to the front door, double checked the "Closed" sign, and locked the door behind her.

Shelly got into her car and drove out of the complex, passing the SUV driven by Hiram just before it pulled into the complex. The SUV took a parking spot reserved for future residents. The undead duo got out, looking dismal in the late morning sunlight. Hiram walked up to the leasing office door and banged on it. Bibi pointed at the sign.

"Being dead affecting your eyesight that bad?"

she asked.

Hiram peered through the windows. "Undead, and no," he replied. "I know this little bitch likes to put that sign up and then go bang whoever's handy in the back room. I was really looking forward to killing her."

"Bust in?"

Hiram shook his head. "The place is alarmed, so that will bring a swifter response from the authorities. I'm not ready to face that mess just yet."

"Well..." Bibi replied as she stepped around the leasing office and looked at the apartment complex. She smiled at Hiram.

"Maybe a complex full of victims will make it up to you?"

Hiram stepped next to her and surveyed the complex. He nodded and smiled. "Yeah, there are some *cabróns* in here who really deserve a life vacation."

They climbed back into the SUV and pulled up to the gate. Hiram punched in the code, leaving an oily, blackish green residue on the buttons. The gate opened, and they drove in.

As they passed the various buildings, Hiram pointed at each building as he slowly drove over the speed bumps.

"Never pick up after their dogs," he said at the first building. "This one's just packed with dealers and pimps–think I'd just like to barricade the doors and light it on fire."

"Lovely neighbors," Bibi commented.

"Decades ago, you used to respect your neighbors. You were considerate, kind and even helpful. Now, they're all just protecting their little fiefdoms and shitting on everyone else," Hiram scoffed. "It isn't even racial. They're all just assholes."

"We have definitely flushed the country into the toilet," Bibi agreed.

"Since they want to let it all go to hell, I say we let them meet *el diablo* faster," Hiram concluded as he pulled into a spot in front of his own apartment building. "We'll start with this little prince of humanity."

They got out of the car and walked up to the second floor. Hiram pounded on a door in the center of the hallway. Loud music blared behind the door.

"Turn that shit down!" Hiram hollered.

From inside the apartment, a muted voice hollered back.

"Fuck you, old man!"

Hiram smiled as he looked at Bibi. "I like this game, but it's going to have a different end today."

Hiram banged on the door again. "I'm gonna call the cops!"

"Shit, that's it!" came the reply from within as footsteps approached the door. "I'm gonna fuck—"

The tenant, Eduardo, dressed in a white tank top and black shorts that hung low on his hips, pulled open the door. As the music blared behind him, Eduardo's face went white when he saw them.

"You up..." Eduardo squeaked out.

Bibi shoved her machete into Eduardo's stomach and he doubled over, hands grabbing at the fresh wound gushing blood down his legs onto the floor. Hiram grabbed Eduardo's hair, pulled his head back, and bit Eduardo's nose off as the struggling man screamed. As Hiram pulled his head away from Eduardo, he turned his head and spit the severed nose out into the complex hallway. Eduardo held one hand to his face and the other to the stab wound in his stomach; he turned to run from his attackers. Bibi shoved her foot into his ass, pushing him forward into his stereo equipment. The music came to a sudden end as electrical sparks flew from the equipment. Eduardo fell to the floor, unconscious or dead; the undead duo wasn't sure which. More blood flowed from a fresh gash on his forehead.

"Music to my ears," Hiram said as he nodded. He perked up and smiled even bigger.

"Let's go visit the *perra* with fifty cats!" he exclaimed.

The helicopter flew over the desert, heading west. Captain Rivas leaned forward and turned his head toward General Brooks.

"Full report on the base and club–both sites fully neutralized," Captain Rivas reported.

"Make a note in Lieutenant Daniels' files for an official reprimand. We should've had the GPS signal on those SUVs hours ago," General Brooks replied.

"On that, sir, GPS still shows the second SUV heading in the general direction of the first one. The first SUV appears to be stopped at an apartment complex, sir."

Brooks put his hands on his face and rubbed his eyes. "Shit," he said as he looked out the window and watched the passing landscape. "Goddamn it, Huckster. Control and contain; not that fucking hard."

General Brooks turned back to Captain Rivas. "Captain?"

"Yes sir?"

"Have Bravo and Charlie contain the apartment

complex and terminate anything that tries to escape," General Brooks said with a deep resignation in his voice.

"Anything, sir?"

Brooks nodded and grimaced. "Yes, Captain. Even the children," he said and turned around and leaned back against the helicopter seat head rest. "Even the children, dammit."

People screamed as they ran from their zombie neighbors that broke through windows in their frenzy to get to their prey. The entire complex was a beehive of mayhem. The fire alarm Hiram had pulled just a few minutes ago had fresh victims coming out from the upper floors to meet undead horrors stalking the hallways.

Bibi and Hiram climbed into the SUV.

"Next stop is my choice," Bibi announced.

Hiram nodded. "Well, it is your turn," Hiram said with a laugh.

"Lazy Ass Bar on Main," Bibi said.

"In Pasadena," Hiram replied with a nod. "It's been a good decade, but I used to know it well."

They drove for the exit. A woman grabbed onto the side of the SUV, pleading for help. Bibi leered at her out the window and swiped at her with the machete. The woman screamed and fell to the asphalt. As they neared the exit, a small child stood in the middle of the chaos, crying. Bibi saw the child as the SUV passed him. Their eyes locked, and she watched in slow motion as a zombie collapsed on top of the child, killing him.

Bibi turned back and stared straight ahead. She grit her teeth as the human being within her struggled to the surface, touched by the child's death. She stabbed the dashboard with the machete, startling Hiram.

"Something wrong?" he asked as they exited the gate.

"It's nothing. Just drive, so we can hurry up and kill the bar trash," Bibi replied quietly.

CHAPTER 18

$\mathcal{D}$eanna kissed Frank at the bar; they were both drunk and sloppily groped each other. Dillon, the bartender, walked up to one of Frank's buddies, Freddy, who was still wearing his work uniform, a utility belt and construction safety vest.

"Looks like it's really happy hour for them," Dillon shouted.

Freddy laughed and pointed at the clock over the bar. "And it's only three o'clock!" Freddy shouted.

Shelly entered the bar and looked around. She spotted her stocky Mexican target, Freddy, at the bar next to the nearly pornographic Frank and Deanna. Shelly licked her lips. *This bar's a bit of a hike*, she thought. *But always worth the trip.*

"Hey, what's your name?" Shelly asked as she sat down next to Freddy.

Freddy looked over from his third beer and grinned. "Hey, my friends call me Freddy, *chica*, but you can call me anytime you want!"

Shelly smiled. "Want to get lucky? I hope you haven't consumed too much *cerveza*," she said, raising an eyebrow.

Freddy frowned. It wasn't the first time a beautiful

woman had walked up to him in a bar and asked him to pay for sex. He sighed.

"I feel like I've seen you here before. How much is this little *fiesta* gonna cost me?" Freddy asked.

Shelly licked her lips seductively and pressed her hand against Freddy's crotch. "Just your time and your sweat, *papi*," she said. She gave him a deep, wet kiss and grabbed Freddy's vest. She dragged Freddy away toward the bathroom with absolutely no protest from him.

"Go Freddy!" The other patrons at the bar cheered for him.

Freddy flipped them the bird before he disappeared with Shelly into the ladies' restroom.

As the restroom door shut, Shelly walked toward the sink counter, swaying her hips seductively. She crooked her finger at Freddy to get him to come to her. Freddy watched her with a widening smile on his face. She hopped up to sit on the counter between the two sinks ringed with rust. She put one of her legs up on the counter, flashing her pink panties below her skirt.

"Now don't disappoint me, Freddy. Show me what kind of man you are."

Freddy slowly walked up to her and pulled her in for another deep kiss. Shelly let her fingers wander below his belt, stroking his rod to firmness. Shelly dropped her leg back down and they made out for several minutes.

"Let's go," she whispered huskily into his ear. Freddy stepped back just a foot or so and reached into his pocket. He pulled out a switchblade and flicked the switch, exposing the blade. Shelly gasped and jumped a little. Freddy reached under her skirt and cut off her panties with a smooth, practiced motion.

"Don't need anything in the way of this love machine, *chica*," Freddy said as he closed the switchblade and put it back in his pocket.

Shelly smiled hungrily, and they resumed their passionate kissing as she fumbled with the button and zipper on his jeans.

General Brooks walked into the hangar. A team of officers and enlisted stood next to a long table in the center of the building.

"SITREP," Brooks stated as he walked up to the table. A major graying at the temples with a high and tight haircut stepped forward and saluted.

"General, we have satellite tracking the two SUVs right now," he said.

"Why haven't we intercepted them yet?" Brooks asked.

"The lead SUV left the apartment complex shortly before we arrived and moved through a residential area on its way to the freeway. We didn't have assets in place to intercept them before they reached the freeway."

"Apartment complex status?" Brooks asked.

"Except for the SUV, we've contained the infection verified by reviewing satellite footage from the start of the infection until our forces arrived on scene. The site…" The Marine cleared his throat and swallowed hard. "Cleansed per orders."

"I understand that was a hard order to carry out, Major Huntington. It was a hard order to give."

"Understood, sir," the junior officer replied with a

clenched jaw. "It's a crime when we do something abroad. I never thought I'd see it here on U.S. soil."

"Neither did I, Major. Neither did I," General Brooks said and stopped to rub his eyes. "Media blackout still in place?"

"It's been challenging, but so far they've been cooperative. We cordoned off a large area around the apartment complex. My understanding is the same is true of the base, strip club and gas station in Nevada."

"These 'operatives' are certainly keeping us on our toes. Now, what's the status of the second SUV?"

"It took a circuitous route directly onto the freeway, bypassing the apartment complex altogether."

General Brooks crossed his arms and looked at the maps laid out on the table in front of him. Each member of the team had computer tablets they worked on as the two officers spoke.

"Any signals?"

"No cell signals or even radio communication between the vehicles, as far as we can tell. However, there was a significant period earlier when they were in the wind. Coordination could have occurred beforehand."

"Assessment?"

"Sir, it appears the occupant of the second SUV either didn't know where the first one was going or they prearranged some kind of rendezvous at a tertiary location."

"Target area?" Brooks asked. Everyone at the table looked up at him.

"We haven't been able to determine that yet. Somewhere north of the apartment complex is all we know. The vehicles are on different highways, so it's difficult to judge exactly where they're going to converge if they're going to converge at all."

"Let's assume they are going to converge. That second SUV wouldn't have come all the way back here if it wasn't trying to catch up to the first one. Nothing else makes sense. When one of them stops for something other than gas, let's get an evacuation corridor around that location for a mile's circumference."

The personnel at the table looked at each other with alarm. "That's going to be extremely difficult in the middle of Los Angeles," one of the older officers at the table said.

"Deploy the National Guard. Tell them a toxic spill has occurred, and the evacuation is urgent. Be sure the commanding officer has a funding account, so there are no delays. Last thing we need is someone scoffing at the cost. This threat has to be eliminated with prejudice. Is that clear?"

Everyone at the table stood up and saluted.

"Let's not let the lives of our fellow countrymen... and children... at that apartment complex have been lost in vain," General Brooks finished and saluted them all. "Now, can someone point me to a coffee pot? It's been a long day."

Major Huntington looked at the personnel at the table and the older man who spoke up earlier nodded his head. "This way, General," Major Huntington said and led the General to an office off to the right.

Hiram pulled up in front of the Lazy Ass Bar right next to the row of motorcycles parked out front. The rhythmic grind of Bibi sharpening her blade permeated the SUV. It was more pronounced when Hiram turned off the engine. "You know we're running on borrowed time. We can't continue to act with impunity," Hiram said. "Eventually, the authorities, whoever they may be, will intercept and stop us."

Bibi stopped sharpening the blade and looked at the edge with a trained eye. She glanced at Hiram and nodded. "I intend to inflict as much damage as possible on this cruel world before I go," Bibi replied. "Although, where we go after this is a mystery. This is where the axe I have to grind ends. There really isn't anything I can think to do after this."

"I have plenty of random targets, but I think I've hit the bulk of mine as well."

"Can you play crowd control while I dissect my chosen victim?"

Hiram looked in the back seat and spotted an automatic rifle. He grabbed the weapon, hunted around, and found a few clips. Bibi looked at Hiram's weapon and smiled. "I'd be delighted. Haven't fired one of these in a few decades, but I don't exactly have to be a marksman in close quarters, do I?"

"Hey, try not to kill them—just wound them. We want a nice collection of mindless zombies left to spread joy and harmony to the world."

Bibi and Hiram got out of the SUV, Bibi sheathed her machete and they walked into the building.

As Bibi walked in, the song playing on the encrusted jukebox just next to the door ended. The door slammed behind Hiram and everyone looked at them.

"Barkeep," Bibi hollered at Dillon, who was just putting clean glasses on a shelf behind the bar. "Better warm up the mop—it's gonna get messy!"

Dillon took one look at Hiram holding the military

assault rifle, whipped out his cell phone and ducked down behind the bar. He dialed 9-1-1, but the call wouldn't go through.

"Fuck!" Dillon hissed at his phone. He looked at the signal and saw no bars of connectivity. "What the hell?"

Frank cocked his head at Bibi and smiled. He pushed Deanna away and turned to face Bibi, his beer still clutched in his left hand.

"Hey, Stumpy," Frank said. He took a swig of his beer. "You look like shit!"

Bibi sauntered up to him as another loud song played on the jukebox.

"Manners, Frankie," Bibi said with a sly grin. She whipped out her machete and hacked off his left hand with one swipe. Frank hollered in pain and grabbed his left bleeding stump with his right hand. When the beer he was holding hit the floor, Bibi held her hand to her lips.

"Party foul," she said. "My bad."

The other bar patrons began moving toward Bibi, but Hiram opened up with his weapon, causing everyone to scramble for cover. He hit a few people who cried out and tried to hide behind the pool table and bar stools; some of them simply fell to the ground.

Frank looked around at everyone being shot. He let out a scream of rage and lunged at Bibi with his right hand. Bibi whipped the machete through the air swiftly, slicing off his other hand. He screamed in pain.

"Who's Stumpy now?" Bibi shouted at him and laughed. She grabbed Frank's hair and pulled him close, sinking her teeth into his throat. He fell to the floor. "Good times, Frankie. Good times."

Deanna rushed at Bibi from the bar, wielding a pool cue. She struck Bib across the back. It broke, leaving Deanna with a busted half of a pool cue. Bibi turned to Deanna and Bibi grinned.

"Leave him alone, you bitch!" Deanna shouted as she waved the stick in front of her.

"Deanna... you always had my back, didn't you?" Bibi said calmly as she advanced on the inebriated woman. Deanna backed away as she swung the stick menacingly in front of her. Bibi kept advancing until Deanna's back hit the bar behind her. Deanna lunged forward and stabbed Bibi in the abdomen.

The cue poked out the back of Bibi's shirt. Bibi grabbed the stick with her right prosthetic hand and swung the machete at Deanna with the left, cutting off Deanna's head.

"Deanna," Bibi said with a laugh. "Always with your head in the gutter..."

As Hiram shot at the bar patrons, knocking them to the ground or leaving them clutching the furniture and walls to stay upright, Bibi wandered around to the stricken, slicing and biting them. One of Hiram's shots hit the music system, ending the musical accompaniment to the slaughter. Within ten minutes, most people were on the floor, dead or dying.

As the pair surveyed their handiwork, Frank sat up, drooling blood and dark green mucus. Approaching sirens drowned out the groans and moans of the dying. Hiram and Bibi turned toward the sound.

"I think it's time we left these good people to their own devices," Hiram said.

Bibi turned and followed Hiram out the door. After a few moments, more of the fallen patrons rose again, their eyes a glazed white as they stumbled around the bar. They latched upon those not yet infected and tore into them. The sounds of screaming and chunks of flesh hitting the walls and floor permeated the hazy room.

Behind the bar, Dillon poked his head up and observed the carnage.

"Shit!" he whispered. He backed away from the carnage, heading for the rear exit when he bumped into someone. He turned around and saw the grinning face of Frank looking back at him, black ichor dripping from his mouth.

"Aw, fuck, Frank," Dillon whimpered before his lifelong friend fell upon him and tore into the hapless barkeep with his teeth.

Inside the ladies' restroom, Freddy pounded away, giving Shelly a good fucking when a zombie entered the bathroom and attacked Freddy, biting him on the shoulder.

"Fuck!" Freddy hollered as he disengaged from Shelly. Freddy spun around, whipped out his switchblade and fought the zombie. Another zombie entered the room and Freddy fought them both off.

Shelly scrambled up to stand on the counter. She climbed out a high window and fell to the ground outside the bar. Getting to her feet, she ran around to the front of the bar. Seeing Bibi and Hiram kicking over bikes, she backed away and ran for an alley across the street.

As the zombies continued to fill the bathroom, Freddy went down amidst a swirl of teeth and fingers clawing at his flesh.

A rocket impacted the SUV in front of Bibi and Hiram before they could reach it. They stood, rooted to the spot, unsure of what to do next. Hiram took aim at the helicopter and fired the assault rifle. A few bullets struck the helicopter, and it quickly flew out of range.

Martin pulled up in the second SUV. "Get in!" he shouted through the open window.

"Martin?!" Bibi shouted with joy as she ran to the SUV. She hugged him through the window. She stepped back and gave him a once over. "Oh, baby," she said. "You don't look so good."

"I'd say we all look like death warmed over. Now get in!" Martin yelled.

Hiram climbed in the back seat while Bibi ran around to the passenger side and climbed in. The SUV sped off as another rocket slammed into the ground nearby. Two more rockets hit the Lazy Ass Bar, and it exploded in a fireball, sending shrapnel flying. Bits of building and chunks of flesh rained down on the SUV before it turned a corner out of sight.

CHAPTER 19

Seeing the two of them back together, Hiram felt the urgency of his blood thirst wane again. Martin's frantic driving, accompanied by Bibi's yelling when the explosions got too close, brought him a sense of peace. He didn't feel renewed desire for Martin's demise, as he was clearly in the same state as the two of them.

He couldn't deny the bloodshed was fun, and he had a genuine sense of curiosity as to how the zombieness of it all worked. But he had to admit, the sense of euphoria and peace that washed over him was welcome. He wondered if this was the precursor to passing over. As the explosions shattered a building to their left and Martin turned a corner to avoid the building's collapse, he bent forward to speak to them.

"Ain't this a blast?" he said to them. They both glanced at him with eyes wide for a moment.

Additional vehicles approached from side streets. Another helicopter appeared, approaching from the north.

"They're boxing us in," Martin announced. He saw a large factory type building ahead and gunned the engine as he headed for one of the rolling doors in the building's side. One last explosion behind them helped propel the vehicle through the door, which crumpled easily under the impact of the SUV. They skidded to a halt in what appeared to be a defunct shipping warehouse undergoing rehab.

They got out of the vehicle and ran to hide behind a large construction dumpster.

General Brooks looked down at the large warehouse the second SUV had disappeared into. He looked at Captain Rivas.

"Lock down the perimeter, one block away. Do not engage," General Brooks said.

"Affirmative," Captain Rivas said as he switched channels and barked orders to the command unit below. As they watched the activity, the various vehicles and personnel set up barricades a full block away.

Martin peered out through the broken door and saw military personnel setting up barricades.

"You got a secret arsenal stashed in here somewhere?" Hiram asked as he walked away from the relative safety of the metal container.

Martin pulled Bibi with him as they went back to the car and put it between them and the military assembling down the street. He put his arms around Bibi and smiled.

"There's no secret stash," Martin exclaimed.

"Then why are we here?" Bibi replied. "We need to get back in the—"

She looked at the SUV and realized the damage to the vehicle was extensive. All the windows were shattered, two of the tires had exploded on impact and there were various fluids leaking from under it onto the bare cement floor.

"We're done," Martin said.

"What?" Bibi asked, and she looked into his eyes.

"Well, shit," Hiram added. He grabbed an abandoned rolling chair and sat down on it. He dropped his weapon to the ground and folded his hands in his lap.

Martin took Bibi's face in his hands. "This isn't who you are. We should be dead. Our time here is over," Martin said simply.

Bibi nodded and hung her head. "I think I knew that when the children died at the apartments. We shouldn't be here anymore. But what about all the zombies we just made?" she asked.

"I think the military has it covered," Martin said as three attack helicopters took position around the building. On the streets below, soldiers took their positions behind cover, weapons trained on the building as they watched for anyone trying to escape.

Bibi and Martin embraced and kissed. It was a wet, sloppy kiss with bits of green and black ooze dripping from their mouths. They pulled back from each other, a little disgusted.

"Maybe we should skip the goodbye kiss," Bibi whispered.

"Yeah," Martin said, as he nodded in agreement.

"Well," Hiram announced from his chair as he leaned back. "It was fun while it lasted."

Martin and Bibi held each other as the rockets let loose from the helicopters. The windows around the building shattered as explosions impacted around the building. An explosion next to the dumpster sent it flying into the air, landing upside down on Hiram, enclosing him and covering him with discarded building materials and trash.

The next three explosions were bombs filled

with napalm.

Bibi and Martin remained in their embrace as they caught fire and eventually burned to cinders in the thousand degree inferno. Minutes later, the weakened warehouse structure collapsed on their cremated remains.

Troops stood outside the Lazy Ass Bar, watching it burn. Screams from inside let them know not everyone dying was a zombie yet.

At the apartment complex, the burning buildings had collapsed to the dark skeletal remains of three-story structures. Some were nothing more than a smoking pile of rubble. Scattered around the buildings, charred remains spread across the surface of the extensive parking lot, the unmistakable remains of human bodies. Additional troops in pairs stood around the perimeter armed with assault rifles and flame throwers, some of them with tears streaming down their faces.

The Double D building was nothing more than a pile of smoking cinder blocks and ash. The lone neon sign in the parking lot was bent over with the sign resting on the pavement next to all the burned-out cars. Soldiers climbed into troop transport vehicles as the fire department arrived. Nothing in or around the smoking debris moved.

EPILOGUE

Shelly limped by the lone car in the parking lot of a small bar across from a closed strip mall. The vehicle was a regular sedan with military stickers on the bumper. She looked at the vehicle and then turned around to look behind her. In the distance, fire rose into the air, lighting up the night sky. The sounds of explosions echoed in the distance.

Shelly walked into the bar and noticed a single customer wearing a loose fitting black hoodie sitting at the far end of the bar nursing a beer in a glass mug. She took a seat close to the door and looked around.

"Where's the bartender?" Shelly asked the lone patron. "I really need a drink."

The patron turned to look at Shelly.

"I think he's taking a nap," Hector replied. Behind the bar, unseen by Shelly, the bartender was face down in a pool of blood.

"Shit," Shelly groaned.

Hector got up from the stool and walked behind the bar, stepping over the body of the bartender.

"It's all right," Hector said as he grabbed a fresh mug and poured her a beer from the tap. He expertly let the foam run off until the mug was full. He walked to her and handed her the mug.

"Hey," Hector said as she took a drink before she looked up at him. "Do you like guys with scars?"